BERKLEY PRIME CRIME
Published by Berkley
An imprint of Penguin Random House LLC
penguinrandomhouse.com

ISBN: 9780593333396

First Edition: May 2022

Printed in the United States of America
1 3 5 7 9 10 8 6 4 2

Strawberried Alive

Jenn McKinlay

BERKLEY PRIME CRIME
New York

For my magical unicorn of a personal
assistant, Christie Conlee,
who brings sunshine and rainbows
wherever she appears.
You simply amaze me,
and I'm so grateful that you
came into my life when you did.
I can't wait to see what we do next!

One

"I'm not paying for these," Emerson Henry snapped. "They're not what I asked for; in fact, they're hideous."

Melanie DeLaura's eyebrows rose up to her hairline. She glanced at the bride-to-be, who stood across the counter from her with her harried mother, Julia Henry, by her side, and debated tossing them out of Fairy Tale Cupcakes. Not to be full of herself but Mel was positive she had never baked a hideous cupcake in her life.

"Now, princess, I don't think—" Julia began, but Emerson interrupted her.

"Exactly. You don't think," Emerson said, with an impatient toss of her long, honey-blond hair. Her wide mouth twisted up into a puckered knot. "I told you to check on the color of the cupcakes, but you said, 'Oh, they'll be fine.' And now look at the mess we're in the day before my wedding. You knew I wanted the cup-cakes to match the new bridesmaids' dresses and these don't. They are aqua and the dresses are teal. Now my wedding is ruined!" Emerson stalked out of the bak-ery, sobbing hysterically and texting frantically as she went.

Julia scrunched up her hands into tight fists. Mel hur-ried around the counter to position herself between the aggravated mother of the bride and the box of cupcakes on the off chance that Julia felt the need to vent her tem-per by slamming her fists into the pastries.

"Twenty-four hours," Julia muttered. She closed her eyes and breathed deeply in through her nose, letting the air out on a soft exhale. Then she gave Mel a small, closed-lip smile. "In twenty-four hours, she will no lon-ger be my problem."

"There's a silver lining," Mel said. "What can I do to help?"

Mel thought about pointing out that if you called your adult daughter "princess" maybe you were part of the problem, but she resisted, guessing that now was not the time, and it really wasn't her business.

She turned to stand beside Julia as they stared down at the cupcakes. They were vanilla cake filled with rasp-berry mousse and topped with white chocolate butter-cream frosting covered with a layer of fondant. The fondant had been matched to the hue of the bridesmaids' dresses with the couple's entwined initials crafted from white chocolate centered on top. Mel plucked a swatch of fabric from where it was taped to the side of the box.

"I gather that Emerson is disappointed, but I don't see how I could match the fondant any more closely than this," she said. She held the fabric against one of the cupcakes and glanced from it to Julia.

Julia rubbed her forehead with her fingers. "That's the original color for the bridesmaids' dresses."

Mel got a sinking feeling in the pit of her stomach. "Original color?"

"Yes," Julia said. "She changed it two weeks ago from aqua to teal and we had to pay an insane amount of money for a rush order on the dresses."

"Oh." Mel had sudden sympathy pangs for the dressmaker and the bridesmaids. "I'm sorry. No one told me."

"Apparently that was my job on top of everything else," Julia said. She sounded bitter and a teeny bit hysterical. She turned troubled eyes to Mel. "Is there any way you can redo the fondant to match the new dress color?" She opened her bag and peered inside. "I have a sample and I'll pay you for your time." She held up the tiny square of teal that was definitely a deeper green than the aqua.

Mel wanted to howl. This would mean an all-nighter and she'd already put in a full day. Given that Emerson had been such a brat, she wanted to say no, but Julia was a longtime customer and other than this wedding, she'd always been a pleasure to work with. Mel didn't want to let her down.

Mel turned to look at her counter help, Marty Zelaznik, who had been listening to the entire exchange. Being an octogenarian who didn't suffer fools, she expected him to have a few choice words to say about the situation. Instead, he raised his hands in surrender and slowly backed away, moving down the counter to help other customers. Mel was on her own.

She glanced at the swatch and then the box of cupcakes. The Henrys had ordered 350, all of which were already boxed and in the walk-in cooler in her kitchen. This was going to mean hours of work. Despite not wanting to do it, she found herself nodding. She couldn't abide the idea of having Emerson Henry trashing her bakery over the color of the cupcakes, because Mel had no doubt that she would, while conveniently leaving out the part that it was completely her own bridezilla fault.

"Okay," Mel said. "I'll have them ready first thing in the morning."

Now Julia looked like she might cry. She pressed the square of fabric into Mel's hands and hugged her. "You're a lifesaver."

Mel watched as Julia rushed out the door after her daughter. She supposed it could be worse. She could be Julia, stuck catering to princess's every whim. Suddenly a night of making new fondant didn't seem so bad.

Marty rang up his customer and joined Mel at the counter.

"Looks like I'm working late," Mel said.

Marty nodded. "'You help the ones you can.'"

Mel gave him side-eye. "Did you just hit me with a movie quote from *Instinct*?"

This had been a long-running game between the bakers, trying to stump each other with movie quotes.

Marty snapped his fingers and looked impressed. "How did you guess it?"

"Please," Mel said. She picked up the box of cupcakes and headed back to the kitchen. "What do you think I am, an amateur?"

He waved a dismissive hand at her just as the bells on

the front door jangled, indicating the arrival of a new customer. Mel left him to it, hoping she had enough ingredients in her stores to handle this massive fondant do-over. She pushed through the swinging door into the kitchen, where she found Angie Harper, one of her partners in the bakery.

"You know, I really never thought that we'd have a high-maintenance bride as hideous as Tate's ex-fiancée," Angie said. She was pacing around the kitchen while trying to rock her six-month-old baby girl, Emari, to sleep. Emari was not having it and instead gurgled at Mel, who was one of her favorite people.

"I assume you were listening at the door?" Mel asked.

"Of course," Angie said. "Princess needs to get over herself."

Mel snorted. She put the box of cupcakes on the table and paused to pat the baby's back and coo at her. Emari had arrived on the scene in a dramatic fashion in the middle of Mel's wedding and she'd been stealing the show ever since with her big brown eyes, downy head of dark hair, and gurgling smiles. Mel loved her as if she were her own, which was not a surprise, given Emari was the progeny of Mel's two best friends.

After being engaged to the wrong woman, Angie's husband, Tate, finally found his Mrs. Right in Angie, who had been waiting for him to notice her since their years as outcasts together in middle school.

Theirs was a true love story and it was one of Mel's favorites, second only to her own. She had recently married her schoolgirl crush, too, who just happened to be none other than Joe DeLaura, the middle of Angie's seven older brothers.

"Dear Joe," as Mel's mother called him, was the love of Mel's life. They were most definitely still in the honeymoon phase of their marriage—so much so, that she hated the fact that she was going to have to work late tonight, when she could be home with Joe and their fur babies: Peanut, their rescue dog, and Captain Jack, their rescue cat. Mel hadn't been looking for pets when they came into her life, but now she couldn't imagine her home without them.

"Do you want me to stay and help?" Angie asked.

Mel shook her head. "No, but thank you. Baby girl needs to go home."

Emari let out a snuffle and nuzzled into her mom's neck. Much as she fought it, sleepiness was winning.

"She does seem to be running the show these days," Angie said.

"Just promise me you won't start calling her 'princess,'" Mel said. "I don't think that pet name works out in the long run."

Angie laughed. "Yeah, no, we'll call her Captain, like Captain Marvel."

"Much better," Mel whispered as Emari's eyes closed and she went limp in her mother's arms, sleep having finally won the battle.

Angie gently placed the baby into her car seat. Emari jerked once when Angie clipped the buckle but didn't wake up. Mel and Angie both sighed in relief. Angie hooked the car seat over her arm and shouldered the diaper bag that went with her everywhere. Mel walked her to the back door to open it for her.

"Call me if you change your mind. Tate has night duty so he won't mind if I come back and help," Angie said.

"Will do," Mel said. She bent down and gently kissed Emari. She stood on the landing behind the bakery and watched as Angie walked to her car, which was parked in the small lot on the other side of the alley. It was still light out but Mel watched her friend until the baby was settled and Angie drove off.

With a sigh, Mel returned to her kitchen and set to work unboxing all of the packed-up cupcakes. She carefully removed the white chocolate initials and set them aside on a sheet of parchment paper, then she scraped off the rejected fondant and most of the underlying buttercream. Using a silicone spatula, she flicked the frosting into a large trash can. She was halfway through when the kitchen door swung open and Olivia Puckett—rival baker and current girlfriend to Marty—appeared. Olivia surveyed the cupcake-covered table and watched Mel scrape another cupcake clean. Then she laughed. It was a full-on belly laugh.

"What happened? Did you mess up an order?"

Mel eyed the gob of frosting on the end of her spatula and debated flicking it at Olivia. Tempting. It was so tempting. Mel lowered the spatula into the trash can and shook the frosting loose. She felt she should get props for being so mature, especially given that dumping the topping in the trash can was not nearly as satisfying as watching a glob of frosting splat her baking rival in the face.

Olivia was still in her chef's coat, having just left her bakery, Confections. She was undoubtedly here to pick up Marty since they lived together. Mel tried not to feel resentful about everyone else having a fun Friday night while she was stuck here. It was a struggle.

7

"No, I didn't mess up," Mel said. "The bride changed her primary color from aqua to teal without telling me until a few moments ago."

Olivia crossed the kitchen to glance at the vast expanse of cupcakes on the table. She let out a low whistle. "That's a lot of boo-boos to fix. Was the bride Emerson Henry by any chance?"

Mel glanced at her in surprise. "How did you know?"

"She came to Confections about her wedding," Olivia said. "Aqua cupcakes with their initials in white chocolate on top, am I right?"

"You're right." Mel gestured to the cupcakes.

"Yeah, we were already booked out," Olivia said. "Now I feel like I dodged a bullet." She patted Mel on the back. Olivia didn't know her own strength—or maybe she did—as the pat almost sent Mel face-first onto the worktable. She caught herself just in time.

"You definitely did," Mel said ruefully. They both studied the sea of cupcakes, acknowledging the amount of work that was ahead of Mel.

"I'd offer to stay and help," Olivia said, "but I don't want to."

That surprised a laugh out of Mel. The door swung open again and Marty appeared. "We're all locked up out front, boss. Liv and I are taking off if you're okay with that?"

"I'm okay," Mel said. She must not have sounded convincing because Marty hesitated, so she added, "Seriously, I'm good. Go, get out of here."

They didn't need to be told twice. The couple crossed through the kitchen and out the back door, which closed with a click of the lock behind them. Mel glanced around her kitchen, which she usually considered her sanctuary, and tried not to resent it.

She turned to her trusty KitchenAid mixer to whip up a fresh batch of fondant. Mel used a gelatin-and-corn-syrup-based recipe, so it wasn't difficult, except that fondant could be persnickety, so she had to mind it carefully. When the rolling fondant had reached the right consistency, she prepped a new batch of white chocolate buttercream.

Mel had a large-screen television mounted on the wall of the kitchen, which she used to watch movies while baking late at night. She flicked through the streaming services until she found a classic—*Bringing Up Baby*. She then picked up her phone and texted Joe, letting him know that she'd be home in a couple of hours. She'd already called to tell him she was working late and he said he and the furry babies eagerly awaited her return. She felt a pang of missing her family. Being married was still very new for her and sometimes she couldn't believe that she was Mrs. Joe DeLaura.

As Kate Hepburn sashayed across the screen, Mel began to pipe fresh buttercream onto the raspberry-filled cupcakes. She supposed she could have baked the cupcakes all over again, but no. Princess of the tantrum did not deserve that much labor from her.

The movie ended and the next one began while Mel worked. *It Happened One Night*, a classic starring Clark Gable and Claudette Colbert, was halfway through when she finished. After she put the last box in the walk-in cooler, she sat down and treated herself to a glass of cold

milk and one (okay, two) of her new favorite cupcakes—
Strawberry Surprise. She and Oscar Ruiz, a former bakery
employee known as Oz, had worked on this recipe until
it was just right. It was packed with real strawberry flavor,
from the cake to the frosting to the chopped-up strawberries tucked into the center. They were ah-mazing. Plus,
Mel figured with all of that strawberry goodness, they
were totally healthy.

She savored each bite and washed them down with
milk. She soon felt her eyes droop. Thankfully, the movie
ended and she had only a couple of miles to drive until
she was home. Mel made quick work of her dishes. She
checked the bakery one more time to ensure everything
was clean, switched off, and put away.

She retrieved her handbag from the tiny corner office
that was formerly a closet and headed out the door. It was
April in South Scottsdale and the nights were still bliss-
fully cool as the heat of the Arizona summer had not yet
arrived. Mel was giddy that she still had to pause to
put on her lightweight hoodie as the chamber of com-
merce weather that was the pride of Arizona was on its
way out.

She zipped up her sweatshirt and ran her fingers
through her short blond hair. She locked the door and
was just setting the alarm on the keypad outside when
she heard footsteps in the alley behind her. Mel froze.

She glanced up at the apartment above the bakery,
where Oz lived. The lights were off. Maybe it was him,
coming home. He was a young man in his twenties. It
wasn't out of character for him to be out this late. Then
again, he was a chef and had to be up when the rooster

crowed to bake his signature desserts for the Sun Dial Resort, where he now worked, so it wouldn't make sense for him to be out at this hour. Oz took his job very seriously.

Mel turned away from the keypad and glanced into the dark alley behind her. She tried to make her voice strong when she called out, "Oz? Is that you?"

In the shadow of the dumpster fifty yards away, she saw a figure dressed all in black. She felt her heart skip a beat—or three. Every instinct screamed at her to get out of there. She tried the handle on the door, but she'd locked it. She fumbled for her keys, wondering if she could get to her car before the person reached her.

"Oz, if you're playing a prank, it's not funny," she cried. *Please let it be Oz, please, please, please.*

There was a sudden boom and the brick beside her arm exploded. *The person had shot at her!* Mel let out a shriek and ducked down behind the railing, as if the skinny wrought iron could protect her from a bullet. From her crouched position, she tried to get the key to the bakery into the lock but her fingers were shaking too hard and she accidentally dropped the keys.

Over the frantic pounding of her heart, she heard the footsteps coming closer. The light over the back door illuminated the area, making it easy for the shooter to see her, but it also helped her spot her keys. She snatched them up and tried the lock again.

Another bullet whizzed through the air and slammed into the metal door above her head, ripping a hole through it. Mel jerked back and curled up into a ball as if she could repel a bullet if she scrunched up tight enough.

The footsteps kept coming and Mel realized this was it. Here on her back stoop, with traces of teal food coloring under her fingernails and the smell of buttercream wafting off her skin like perfume, she was about to die.

TWO

"Hey!" A shout sounded from above at the same time that a potted plant went flying through the air in the direction of the shooter. It hit the pavement right in front of the person in black and shattered, the shards exploding in every direction.

There was a yelp and then the sound of pounding footsteps as the person ran away. Mel glanced up to see Oz bolting down the steps from the landing above. He dropped to his knees beside her and asked, "Are you hurt?"

"No." She shook her head.

"Are you sure?"

"Y-yes." She nodded. Her teeth were chattering.

"All right, wait here," he said.

Before Mel could stop him, Oz jumped off the stoop and sprinted after the shooter.

"Oz!" Mel cried. She jumped to her feet. "Stop! Don't chase him! Oz, wait!"

He disappeared into the shadows and Mel scrambled to get her phone out of her bag and call the police. Jumping the line, she called her uncle Stan, who was a homicide detective with the Scottsdale Police Department. He answered on the second ring.

"Are you okay?" he said.

Uncle Stan always sounded tense when she called, as if expecting bad news. She hated to confirm his fear but there was no candy-coating this situation.

She took a shaky breath and said, "Someone shot at me while I was closing up the bakery. Can you send a car over? Also, Oz chased after the shooter and I'm worried about him. They were headed down the alley that opens up onto Main Street."

"Where are you now?"

"Back stairs of the bakery," she said. "Exactly where I was when they shot at me."

"Go inside," Stan said. She could hear him moving and knew he was already about to head out the door. "I have to step out, babe. Back in a sec."

"I'll keep your side of the bed warm."

Mel recognized her mother's voice in the background, except she didn't sound like her mother. The voice was low and sultry and—oh, mercy, she'd called Uncle Stan while he was in bed with Joyce. *Gah!*

"Sorry," Mel said. She felt her face get warm as if she were thirteen instead of thirty-plus years old. "I probably should have called dispatch."

"No," Uncle Stan said. "It's good that you called me. Are you inside yet?"

Mel picked up her keys and unlocked the door. Then she disarmed the alarm on the keypad. She glanced one more time down the alley for Oz before she stepped inside and closed the door. She moved to the window to watch for Oz. There was no sign of him.

"I am now," she said.

"Get away from the window," Uncle Stan said.

How did he know she was looking out the window? She heard an engine start in the background and knew he was in his car.

"Call Joe," he said. "I'm going to radio for some patrol cars. If Joe doesn't answer, call me right back. I want you in contact with someone at all times. Got it?"

"Got it," Mel said. The call ended and she used the voice command to call Joe.

"Hey, cupcake, are you on your way home?" he asked.

His deep voice was so reassuring, Mel felt her spine relax for the first time since she spotted the person in black.

"I'm going to be late, I'm afraid," she said.

There must have been something in her voice because his tone changed from warm affection to tight concern in a blink.

"What's wrong? Are you all right? Where are you?" he asked, without giving her a chance to answer.

"I'm fine," she said. She heard a door slam and knew he was headed for his car. She took a quick breath and tried to sound more at ease than she felt. "I just . . . there was . . . when I was locking up . . ."

"You're killing me, cupcake," he said. "Just tell me what happened in as few words as possible."

"Someone shot at me when I was locking up the bakery," she said.

"*What?!*" he cried. Mel heard a car engine rev. "Where? How?"

"Do not speed, Joseph DeLaura. You're no good to me if you get into an accident," she said.

"What happened?" He sounded exasperated.

Mel described the attack, sticking just to the facts.

"Did you call the police?" he asked.

"I called Uncle Stan," she said. "He's on his way and was going to call in some patrol cars." A siren could be heard in the distance. "I bet that's them."

"Do not go outside," Joe said. "And stay away from the window."

He sounded like Uncle Stan. Mel rolled her eyes.

"Joe, Oz scared off the shooter by throwing one of his potted plants at him, but then he chased after him. He hasn't come back. I'm worried."

"Don't be," he said. "Oz is as tough as they come and he's not stupid. He'll be all right."

Mel started to pace. Her hand was shaking and sweat slicked her palm, making it hard to keep a grip on her phone. "I hope so."

"Tell me everything you can remember," Joe said. "I want to hear it while it's fresh in your mind."

Mel repeated what she'd told him, including every detail she could think of, pausing only once, when Joe cursed at the car in front of him for not moving on the green light fast enough.

There was a rap on the back door. Mel glanced through

the window and saw two uniformed officers standing on the steps with Uncle Stan.

"The cavalry has arrived," she said. "I'm going to let them in."

"Uncle Stan is there, too?" Joe clarified.

"Yes," Mel said.

"Okay, I'm a minute out," he said. "I'll see you in a few."

Mel ended the call and hurried to open the door. Uncle Stan was examining the bullet-damaged brickwork while the uniforms waited at the bottom of the stoop.

"Hey, Uncle Stan," Mel said. She glanced at the wall, noted the missing chunk from the bullet, and felt her knees go weak. "Do you want to come in?"

"Hey, kiddo," Uncle Stan said. He paused and pulled her into a reassuring bear hug, a specialty of the Cooper men. He released her and patted her shoulder. "You good?"

Mel nodded. She gestured to the door. "Did you notice this one?"

Uncle Stan frowned and let out a low whistle. "How close?"

"It missed me by a couple of feet," Mel said. She crouched down and said, "I was down here and the shooter was standing right where that potted plant is smashed on the ground over there."

Uncle Stan studied the two locations and nodded.

"So, we're not dealing with a skilled marksman, unless they weren't actually trying to kill you but just scare you," he said. He gestured to the uniforms to join him on the landing. "See how this bullet went right through the door? I want you to go inside and see if you can find it.

Then I want you to come back outside and walk the area. Maybe we'll get lucky and the shooter will have dropped something personal."

"Like his wallet."

"Or his phone."

"Yeah, along with his pet unicorn," Uncle Stan said. His tone was not optimistic. He made a shooing gesture with his hands. "Get to work."

"Yes, sir," they answered in unison.

Mel stepped aside so that the officers, a man and a woman, could enter the bakery. They both pulled blue latex gloves out of their back pockets and tugged them onto their fingers as they entered the kitchen.

"If you find the bullet, don't touch it," Uncle Stan said. "Call me."

"Yes, sir."

Uncle Stan looked at Mel. "Is it just me or do these rookies get younger and younger every year?"

Mel smiled. "It's not you."

With the officers inside, Uncle Stan gave her the once-over. "Are you sure you're okay? I didn't tell your mother where I was going because I didn't want her to worry, but you should probably call her."

"You want me to get you out of trouble for not telling her where you were going," Mel said. Uncle Stan looked sheepish. Mel shook her head. "Have you even met my mother? She is going to be furious when she finds out it was me you rushed off to help without saying anything. Whether I call her or not, your side of the bed is going to be ice-cold."

Uncle Stan's face went bright red. "You heard that?"

"Uh-huh," Mel said. She knew she was enjoying his

discomfort more than she should but she couldn't help herself. Uncle Stan was her late father's younger brother. When Charlie Cooper had teed off to the big fairway in the sky, Stan had stepped up and been the father figure Mel and her brother, Charlie, had needed. After a decade of looking after his brother's family, Stan had started dating Mel's mother, Joyce. While it had taken Mel a minute to get used to the idea, it felt right somehow.

"Mel!" A voice shouted her name and Mel glanced over her shoulder to see Joe running toward her. Behind him limped a wheezing Oz. Relief rushed through her at the sight of her former sous chef, alive and well, and she reached out to grab Uncle Stan's arm in a tight grip to steady herself.

"Thank goodness," she said. She'd been terrified that he might have actually caught up to the shooter and been shot.

She was about to reprimand Oz for running off, but Joe dashed up the steps, snatched her close in a crushing hug, and then kissed her soundly on the mouth. Then he patted her down as if he was looking for a bullet hole or a leak.

"I'm okay," she said. She caught his hands in hers, squeezed his fingers, and stared into his eyes. "I promise. I'm fine."

Joe nodded. He glanced at Uncle Stan, who was watching them in amusement, as if he hadn't just squeezed the stuffing out of Mel, too.

"You, on the other hand, are in big trouble, buster," Mel said as she turned on Oz, who was drenched in sweat and breathing heavily.

"I met him in the parking lot on his way back," Joe said. "He's all right."

Oz bent over, still wheezing, and braced himself while he sucked in big gulps of air.

"He doesn't look all right," Mel said. "Why is he limping?"

"Twisted . . . my . . . ankle . . ." Oz gasped.

"Oh, no! You have to sit," Mel said. She hurried down the steps and put Oz's arm over her shoulders and signaled for Joe to do the same on his other side. "We'll help you inside."

Oz opened his mouth but Mel said, "No arguing. You scared four years off me. What were you thinking, chasing after a person with a gun? You could have been shot and maimed or murdered. Then what would you do?"

"Should I just let her get it out of her system?" Oz asked Joe.

"I find that's usually best," Joe said.

"Do not patronize me," Mel said. She glanced at her uncle as they hobbled toward the stairs. "Tell him I'm right. He was crazy to go chasing after a person with a gun."

"She's right. That was dumb," Uncle Stan said. "But did you catch up to the suspect? Did you see anything that might help us locate them?"

"Uncle Stan!" Mel protested.

They all ignored her as Oz nodded. "The shooter got away from me and I didn't see much. He was dressed all in black and his build was medium all over. There was nothing exceptional about him—even his shoes were generic black running shoes. But I did see the car he was driving. It was a dark—blue or black—BMW sedan and the license plate ended with N8."

Uncle Stan clapped Oz on the shoulder. "Nice work. Go get that boy a cupcake."

Mel gave him a withering look.

"Sorry, but you have to admit that's a solid lead."

"I admit nothing except that it was a foolish risk to take," Mel said. "Come on, let's get him inside."

"I can walk," Oz said.

Mel and Joe ignored him, helping him up the stairs whether he liked it or not.

Uncle Stan held the door open as they turned sideways to drag Oz over the threshold. The two officers were on the far side of the kitchen. They were examining a hole in the wall.

"Looks like we found it, Detective," the female officer said. Her badge read *A. Margolis.*

"It appears to be imbedded in a stud," the male, *B. Salazar*, added.

Uncle Stan approached them. He glanced at Mel and Joe and said, "Why don't you park him at a table in front?"

Joe looked like he'd protest but Mel led the way through the swinging doors to the customer side of the bakery, giving him no choice but to help her.

"Really, I've got this," Oz protested. Again, they ignored him.

As soon as they sat Oz in a chair at a table, Joe headed back into the kitchen. Mel was about to follow when he turned and blocked her. "Stay here and take care of Oz."

"I'm fine," Oz said, still panting for breath.

Mel wanted to argue and Joe must have seen it on her face because he said, "Stan will talk more freely to me if you're not there."

There was no arguing the point. Joe was right. Mel gave him a surly glance and he smiled in understanding. "I'll tell you everything I learn."

Mel stared at him.

"I promise," he said with his hand over his heart.

Mel turned back to Oz, pushing an empty chair in his direction. "Put your foot up. Do you want some ice for your ankle?"

"It'll be fine," he said. With a wince he lifted his leg onto the chair. "I'm more worried about the sad state of my lung capacity. I could not catch up to that guy."

"For which I am ever grateful," she said. "He had a gun, Oz."

Oz gave her a look that clearly said *Duh*. Mel threw her hands in the air and plopped down in the seat across from him.

"I'm serious, Oz," she said. "That was a bad call."

He shrugged. "Admittedly, I didn't think it through but on the upside at least we've got a partial plate."

"Not worth your life," she said.

Oz rolled his eyes. Her mother-henning was clearly exasperating to him but Mel couldn't help it. Oz had come to work at the bakery as an intern when he was at the local tech high school. After graduating culinary school, he had left the bakery to carve out his own path, which was fine as he was still close by in Mel's old apartment above the bakery.

She'd always been grateful to have him keep watch over the place but now she wondered if it was such a great idea for him to be living here by himself. Yes, he was big and strong and a full-grown man, but she'd never forgive herself if something happened to him.

"I think maybe you should stay somewhere else for a while," she said. "Maybe you could move home for a few weeks."

Oz lifted one perfectly shaped eyebrow. Since he'd starting doing segments for the Foodie Channel, he was more immaculately groomed than Mel or Angie had ever been with his clean-shaven, tiny-pore, perfect skin. Truly, he'd always been a handsome kid but he had become quite the looker in front of the camera. He'd even begun to fret about his hairline, which was ridiculous but Mel supposed the constant media scrutiny would do that to a person. He'd recently taken Marty to a spa day, which would live in infamy as Marty had gotten into a tussle with his masseuse over his towel placement. Apparently Marty had been going for a stuffed-burrito look, with his towel covering him from neck to knee, and the masseuse wasn't having it.

"Don't look at me like that," Mel said. "We have no idea who the shooter was or whether they'll come back or not. You living here alone is not safe."

"They were chased off easily enough by a flowerpot, so it was a pretty lame attempt at a robbery. Why do you think they'd come back?" Oz asked.

"Because it probably wasn't a robber," Uncle Stan said as he pushed through the door to reenter the kitchen.

"Stan," Joe said. His voice was full of warning. He was right behind the detective, looking grim, and Mel knew that the bullet in the kitchen had clearly upset him.

"What?" Uncle Stan asked.

"Maybe I should be the one to share your theory," Joe said.

"Why you?"

"Because I'm a bit more tactful than you."

"Enough, you two," Mel said. "Just spit it out."

"All right, I think it was probably someone coming to kill you," Uncle Stan said.

Three

Mel frowned. She held up one hand. "Hang on. I think I'm going to need a cupcake."

A normal person might have felt that the two cupcakes she'd already consumed would sit in her gut like a sugary dough ball. Not Mel. Cupcakes were comfort. They soothed her in times of stress. Since she'd already made healthy choices she was going full on for a double chocolate cupcake with coconut buttercream on top.

She entered the kitchen, which was empty as the officers were outside scouting the area, and headed right for the walk-in cooler. Using one of the serving trays they used for dine-in customers, she loaded up a platter full of cupcakes and some glasses of milk, putting some aside for Margolis and Salazar when they returned, and headed back to the kitchen.

Joe and Uncle Stan were seated at the table and they all made room for Mel to put down her tray. She had loaded other flavors—red velvets, s'mores, limoncello, and champagne-flavored cupcakes—knowing it would cover all of the flavor cravings of their group. The champagne ones felt appropriately light, given that she'd already had two Strawberry Surprise cupcakes, but she went for the chocolate and coconut instead.

They each grabbed a cupcake and Mel looked at Uncle Stan. "Okay, explain."

"Not much to say, really." He shrugged. "You're now married to an assistant district attorney. Anyone has a beef with him and you make a pretty good target for revenge."

"That's it," Joe said. He took a huge bite of a limoncello cupcake, practically swallowing it whole, as if it was a stress reliever. "You're going to stay with your mom."

"No, I'm not," Mel said. Joe furrowed his brow in his trademark stubborn look. Mel glanced at Uncle Stan and added, "That could potentially put my mom in danger and we can't have that."

Stan nodded. "She's right."

"No one would know she was there," Joe argued. "We could sneak her in and keep her hidden."

"What are you going to do, lock me in a closet?" Mel asked.

Joe didn't answer and she shook her head at him.

"No, it's too big of a risk," she said. "Besides, we have no idea who the shooter was or why they shot at me. It might have nothing to do with me. It could have been a random robbery."

"Why would anyone rob a cupcake bakery?" Stan

asked. He bit into his red velvet and heaved a sigh of contentment. "I mean, I love cupcakes, but it's not like it's a jewelry store or an art gallery with valuable merchandise."

Mel gave him a look and he shrugged.

"He does have a point," Oz said. "It's not like we're cash heavy, and our product is a consumable, so not exactly theft-worthy."

Mel turned her glare on him.

Joe patted her shoulder and said, "I'd rob the place for the cupcakes."

Mel gave him a small smile. "That's not really a surprise, given your legendary sweet tooth."

They ate in silence for a while. Finally, Uncle Stan dabbed his mouth with his napkin and said, "Aside from a criminal who's out to hurt your husband, you've been involved in a number of murder investigations, Mel. People have been sentenced to years in jail because of you."

The coconut frosting in Mel's mouth suddenly tasted as appetizing as kale. She swallowed and it went down hard. "What are you saying?"

"That there are a lot of people out there who may have a vendetta against you," he said.

"Yeah," Oz agreed. "And not just the people who got put away but their families, too. If you think about it, there could be dozens of people who want you dead."

Mel tipped her head to the side. "Not really helping, Oz."

"Sorry," he said.

Joe said, "So, we need to track down each of these people and their families and find out if any of them drive a black four-door sedan with the last digits on the license plate N8." He glanced at Stan. "Is that something the department can do?"

"We can," he said. "It may take more time than if we hire an independent investigator, as our officers have other cases they're working."

"I might have someone who'll do," Joe said.

Uncle Stan met his gaze and a look of understanding passed between them. Uncle Stan nodded. "Bring him on board, but tell him not to push it. Everything has to be by the book."

"Got it."

"Bring who on board?" Mel asked.

But Uncle Stan had already moved on to his next concern.

"We also need to look at your convictions," Uncle Stan said to Joe. "You've put away a lot of bad guys in your years as a prosecutor and as Oz pointed out, it might not be the guys behind bars but the people who were left behind—families, friends, associates."

Joe ran a hand over his face. He looked weary and Mel wanted to hug him. Instead, she handed him another cupcake and said, "I doubt it's one of your cases. They'd probably just go after you. I still think it was a random happenstance. Wrong place, wrong time. Unless they were casing the bakery, they'd have had no way of knowing I was going to be working late tonight. And if it wasn't random, then I think Uncle Stan is right and it's probably one of the murder investigations I've been tangled up in over the years."

"Weirdly, that doesn't reassure me at all," Joe said. He bit into his cupcake.

"You know, by and large, criminals are dumb," Uncle

Stan said. "I mean, these are people who think cheating is getting ahead so long as you don't get caught. They believe it's their right to take what they want when they want it, again, so long as they get away with it. The shooter could be a lone bad guy who was up to no good and shot at you because they panicked when you stepped out of your bakery. As you said, it's possible it has nothing to do with you except bad timing."

Mel nodded eagerly. She liked this scenario. This one made sense to her and didn't frighten the bejeezus out of her.

"But that's not likely," Joe added.

Mel sighed. "So what do we do now?"

"Gather evidence, canvass the area, and try to identify the shooter," Uncle Stan said. "In the meantime, everyone has to be on high alert."

Mel looked at Joe and said, "Angie and the baby can't be here for a while."

"Agreed," he said.

"And I'm not sure about the rest of the staff, either," she said.

"We'll post security at the front and back entrances," Uncle Stan said. "I'll keep some squad cars parked around the building. Best deterrent in the world."

"Thanks, Uncle Stan," Mel said. She gave him a quick hug.

Oz swallowed his last bit of cupcake and said, "You know, it could be that I've been working at the resort with some rather high-maintenance clientele, but I have to ask—you don't have any extremely overwrought customers who might be angry with you over a special order or anything like that, do you?"

29

"N—" Mel paused.

Today's high-maintenance bride, Emerson, might still be a bit miffed with her about the cupcake colors, but since Mel was fixing them, she really couldn't see why. Plus, Emerson's big day was tomorrow—could she really be shooting at Mel the night before her wedding? Nah.

"Who are you thinking about?" Joe asked.

"No one in particular," Mel said. "I mean, there are always people who complain or give the random lousy online review, but I can't think of any situation where it escalated to the point of them wanting to shoot me."

"What about that lady who wanted a life-size rendering of herself in her wedding dress made out of cake?" Oz asked.

Mel groaned. She was never going to forget that one. The woman had threatened to burn the bakery down if she didn't comply. Mental.

"That was two years ago," she said. "She must be over it by now."

Oz shrugged.

"Name?" Uncle Stan asked.

"Kerry Crenshaw," Mel said. "Although, she was marrying a guy named Hoover, so she might be Kerry Hoover."

Uncle Stan used his phone to make a note.

"I really don't think it's her," Mel said.

"What if her marriage didn't work out?" Oz asked. "Maybe she blames it on you and your lack of cake."

"That'd be insa—" Mel stopped speaking because the insane part actually fit Kerry very well. Mel had refused to make the cake she requested primarily because the turnaround time wasn't enough but also because she suspected that Kerry would be the sort of customer who could never be pleased and Mel had hit a place in her career where she just didn't have time for that. "Yeah, I guess it wouldn't hurt to talk to her."

"Anyone else?" Uncle Stan asked.

"How about the man who refused to pay for half of the three hundred cupcakes he ordered for his retirement?" Joe asked. He looked at Uncle Stan and said, "Only one hundred and fifty guests showed up, so he wanted to return the uneaten cupcakes and get a refund."

"Oh, that guy," Mel said. The mere thought of him gave her a headache. "Richard Nordquist. He showed up here every day for two weeks demanding his money back for the uneaten cupcakes. As if we could take back and sell cupcakes that had been sitting out on a table for five hours." Mel rolled her eyes.

"I remember that episode," Oz said. "By the second week, I thought Marty was going to take him out."

Mel laughed.

"How'd you finally get rid of him?" Uncle Stan asked.

Mel and Oz exchanged a look. "It could be that a certain brother paid him a visit at his retirement community and encouraged him to find some new hobbies."

"You never told me about that," Joe said. "I assumed he just moved on."

"Whiners never move on," Oz said.

Mel shrugged. "I only found out about it after the fact."

"Let me guess which brother—Ray?" Uncle Stan asked.

Ray DeLaura was the black sheep of the DeLaura family and he and Uncle Stan had what Mel considered to be a complicated relationship, especially since Ray was dating Uncle Stan's partner, Detective Tara Martinez.

Mel didn't want to rat him out but it was so obviously something Ray would do, so she nodded.

Uncle Stan added a note to his phone. "Any other customers have a grudge with the bakery?"

Mel and Oz exchanged a look. They both shook their heads. "Not that I can think of," Mel said.

"Me, either," added Oz. "But Angie and Marty might remember different ones and I suppose we could ask Tate if he's had any issues with the franchises."

Fairy Tale Cupcakes had independent shops all over the country, which was Tate's job to manage, as their resident financial wizard.

"But given that Tate is the front man, wouldn't anyone with an issue go after him?" Joe asked.

"Maybe." Mel shrugged. "But we are the flagship bakery so if they were truly crazed they might come after one of us here."

"I still prefer the original theory that you walked out of the bakery at the wrong time," Oz said.

"Me, too," Mel admitted. She studied him. "Are you sure you'll be okay up in your apartment? You're welcome to stay with me and Joe."

She glanced at Joe and saw him nod. "We have the room."

Oz gave them a small smile. "Thanks, but I'm fine. I doubt they'll come back tonight. I know I made contact when I tossed my plant at them, which is annoying because it was my heartiest mint plant." He looked at Mel. "You know how I feel about fresh ingredients."

"They're the best," she agreed. "Nice throw, by the way."

"Pure adrenaline," he said. "And a little rage."

Uncle Stan clapped him on the shoulder. "If you hear anything suspicious tonight, you call me directly." He handed Oz his card. "And you do not, under any circumstances, chase anyone down. Understand?"

"Got it," Oz said. "I don't think I could with this ankle, anyway."

"Come on," Joe said. "I'll help you up the stairs."

"I don't need—" Oz said but Joe was already hauling his arm over his shoulders.

"I'll be right back," Joe said.

Mel nodded. She waved to Oz and said, "If you change your mind, call us anytime and we'll come get you."

Oz grunted as he put some weight on his foot, leaning heavily on Joe as they left the front of the bakery and crossed through the kitchen. Mel had a feeling Joe was going to tuck him in with some pain reliever and that was going to be it for Oz for the evening.

"You're lucky he was home and that he has a good arm," Uncle Stan said. They followed Joe and Oz to the kitchen, watching as they exited the bakery and climbed the stairs to the apartment above.

"Thanks for coming over so fast," she said. "What are you going to tell Joyce?"

"The truth," he said. He ran a hand over his face. "I expect it will be a long evening."

The back door opened and Margolis and Salazar joined them. Mel offered them cupcakes, which they gratefully consumed while they reported to Uncle Stan about what they'd found, which was a lot of nothing.

"Most of the businesses are closed," Margolis said. "The only one who still had a person on the premises was

33

the cold-pressed soap shop next door. Naomi Sutter? Yeah, she heard the gunshots but thought it was a car backfiring."

Salazar shrugged. "She didn't even look outside when she heard the noise."

"Naomi." Mel nodded. That made sense, seeing as Naomi was the owner of Naomi's Natural Soap. Mel had met her new neighbor a few times. Naomi was friendly and enthusiastic. She popped in every now and then for a cupcake. Mel had done the same and bought some of her soap. It was divine.

Naomi had been in business next door for only about six months. She'd taken her online business and brought it to a brick-and-mortar location. She'd admitted it was a gamble but she was very determined.

Her shop smelled amazing and she did live demonstrations of her cold-pressed soap process, which fascinated Mel. Naomi kept long hours. In fact, she was one of the only other local business owners whom Mel saw working as late as she did.

Mel made a mental note to pop in and see Naomi tomorrow. Because she was new, Mel wanted to assure her that late-night shootings were very, very rare in this part of town. And if she got lucky, maybe Naomi would remember something by then that might help them discover who the shooter was.

\\\'/\\/\\\\

Surprisingly, Mel crashed into a deep, dreamless sleep and woke up late, at seven o'clock, the next morning. She noted that Joe was already out of bed and the pets were gone, too. She popped up, quickly made the bed, and hurried to the kitchen. She was usually up at six and at work by seven. Julia was going to pick up the cupcakes early today and Mel wanted to be at the shop when she did in case there was more fallout . . . okay, more accurately, she wanted the praise for saving the day because those cupcakes looked spectacular, if she did say so herself.

She hurried into the kitchen to find Joe leaning against the counter, absently petting Captain Jack, so named because he had a black patch of fur over one eye, which made him look like a pirate.

Peanut, their Boston terrier, was outside with her nose to the ground, sniff-patrolling the backyard, looking for signs of any interlopers who may have visited in the night.

"Mornin', cupcake," Joe said. "I was about to bring you this."

He handed her a cup of coffee fixed just the way she liked it, with a teaspoon of sugar and a dollop of milk. Mel kissed him quick and then wrapped her hands around the steaming mug.

"Thanks, but why didn't you wake me?" she asked. "I'm going to be late."

Joe studied her over the rim of his own mug. He looked as if he was trying to figure out what to say.

"What?" she asked. She narrowed her eyes. "What is going on in that attorney brain of yours? Because you're freaking me out."

"Uncle Stan and I had a talk this morning," he said.

Mel held up her hand in a wait gesture and took a restorative sip. She suspected she was going to need it.

"Continue," she said.

"Until we know more about the shooter and their purpose, we don't think you should go into the bakery."

"At all?" she asked.

He nodded.

Mel took a breath in through her nose. She held it for a moment. Then she let it out in a slow, steady exhale. She was fairly even tempered but this "decision" by the men in her life was pushing all of her buttons.

"I appreciate that you are concerned," she said.

Joe's shoulders relaxed as if he was relieved that she was being reasonable.

"But I'm not staying home," she said.

His shoulders jerked back up.

He opened his mouth to argue but Mel shook her head. "As you pointed out, we don't know what the shooter's purpose was and until we do, I can't ignore my business on the off chance that the shooter was gunning for me."

"Cupcake." Joe said the endearment in that charm-laden way he had that usually made Mel feel all swoony and agreeable. Not today.

"Don't you 'cupcake' me," she said. "I have spent years building my business and I'm not going to abandon it now because maybe someone is out to kill me. Big maybe."

"I thought you might feel that way, so if you insist on going into the bakery, there are going to be conditions," Joe said. He crossed the kitchen to the sliding glass door. He slid it open and said, "Come on in."

Mel glanced down at her sleepwear, a unicorn T-shirt and matching pink and gray plaid flannel pajama bottoms, and wondered whom Joe could possibly be inviting into their home when she still had bedhead, not nearly enough caffeine, and a one-horned mythical beast on her chest.

The buzz cut gave it away immediately. Dwight Pickard. Mel sighed as her former high school nemesis stepped into the house with Peanut on his heels, barking in welcome.

Four

Mel frowned and said, "Dwight, what are you doing here?"

"Good morning to you, too," he said. He grinned at her as if enjoying her discomfort. He took in the pajamas at a glance. "Aren't you a newlywed? What are you trying to do, scare him off?"

Mel glared and turned to Joe. "Explain."

"Bodyguard."

"You have got to be kidding me."

His face was as serious as a flour shortage.

"Joe, no." Mel shook her head. "I do *not* need a body-guard."

"Uncle Stan and I disagree," he said.

"Well, it's a good thing I'm a grown woman with my

own opinion and autonomy, isn't it?" she asked. She turned to Dwight. "Great seeing you, but we're not going to need your services as a bodyguard."

Dwight was a tall man, built broad, with a square jaw and a stubborn brow, the sort of guy who looked like he'd be most at home under the hood of a car or swinging an ax, not trailing after a cupcake baker in her bakery while waiting for a random shooter to possibly appear.

"You're cute," Dwight said. "You sound like you think you actually have a choice."

"I do," Mel said.

"You don't," Joe said.

Mel went rigid. She wasn't sure she liked this side of husband Joe. He seemed rather bossy and who did he think he was, telling her what she could or couldn't do? She'd built her bakery from scratch by herself—okay, with a financial boost from Tate—but still it was her blood, sweat, and tears, her recipes, her hours spent creating the perfect cupcakes. She opened her mouth to argue but Joe cut her off.

"Dwight is studying cybersecurity at ASU—they have a top-rated program," he said. "So, he's not just a bodyguard. He's got skills."

Mel blinked at him.

"There's a fortune to be made in cybersecurity," Dwight said. "And I am just the man to make it."

Mel ignored him and turned to Joe. "Okay, what does that have to do with him being my big, overgrown shadow?"

"The time he'll spend with you in the bakery as your body . . . er . . . guarding your person, he'll also be researching the people who you've helped put behind bars over the past few years to figure out where they are and whether they're out to cause you any harm."

"You can do that?" Mel asked Dwight.

Dwight cracked his knuckles, wiggled his fingers, and smiled, showing all of his teeth. "Let me at 'em."

"All right," Mel agreed. She'd been outmaneuvered and she knew it. She turned to Joe. "You win." He smiled. She then turned to Dwight and said, "But if you're hanging out in the bakery you're going to have to wear an apron and look like staff."

"No."

"Yes."

They held each other's gaze. It was a standoff. Mel grinned without blinking. She, Tate, and Angie had perfected the staredown as kids, and she could do this all day.

"I have to say the hot pink really brings out the ruddiness in your cheeks," Marty said. He batted his eyelashes at Dwight, who responded with a low growl.

"At least I have a full head of hair," Dwight retorted. He tied the apron strings around his middle, looking suitably masculine despite the embroidered cupcake on the bib.

Marty gasped and tossed his head as if there were a thick wavy mane on his bald dome. They were standing in the front room of the bakery, which thankfully didn't have any customers at this early hour.

"Enough, you two," Mel said. "We don't want to

taint our business with all of this testosterone-fueled bickering."

She waved her hands as if trying to dispel some bad fumes.

"He started it," Dwight said.

"Really?" Mel said. "How old are you?"

"Not *that* old," Dwight said. He gave Marty a side-eye.

"That's right, you're not, so show an elder some respect," Marty retorted.

"I will when I see one who's worthy."

Marty glared. "My baby toe is more worthy than you'll ever be."

"Nope." Dwight shook his head.

"It is!" Marty insisted. He bent over and started to untie his shoe.

"Marty, no," Mel said. She had no idea what taking off his shoe would prove but she was not having his bare feet in her bakery. "Shoes stay on."

"Fine," he said at the same time Dwight muttered, "Coward."

Marty puffed up like a wet rooster. "You are!"

Mel clapped a hand to her forehead. "Stop!" She pointed at Marty. "You get behind the counter and greet the incoming customers and you"—she paused to point at Dwight—"get in the kitchen and start doing your cyber whatever it is on the computer and do not speak to each other again. Am I clear?"

Both men nodded and went their separate ways. Mel had a feeling this was going to be a long couple of days. At least she hoped it was only a few days. Surely, they'd know who the shooter was soon. They had to, as having

Dwight shadow her every move was going to get old very fast.

Dwight seated himself at the worktable and tapped away on his laptop while Mel worked on the stock she'd baked for the display cases. She'd decided to bake some Hummingbird Cupcakes because she loved the cream cheese frosting that decorated the tops of them. It had a lovely glossy sheen and she topped each one with half of a toasted pecan.

Dwight glanced at the pad of paper at his side. He ran his finger down the list of names. "You sure have a lot of enemies, Cooper. Why am I not surprised?"

"It's DeLaura now," Mel said. Dwight rolled his eyes. "And what do you mean you're not surprised? It's not like I've done anything to warrant making enemies."

"Please, I've known you since high school," he said.

"Where I did *nothing*," she said. "No clubs, no activities, no cliques, no boyfriends—really, how could anyone have an issue with me? I was practically invisible."

"Haven't we covered all of this old ground before?" he asked.

Dwight had come back into Mel's life during their fifteenth high school reunion. He had been one of the chief tormentors of her existence back in the day, and Mel marveled that they'd been able to bury the hatchet, although if he kept it up, she was going to bury it right in his thick skull.

"Um . . . you brought it up," she said.

"How do you figure?" He looked genuinely perplexed.

"You said you weren't surprised that I have so many enemies," she said. She gathered her ingredients and began to measure them out before turning around to face him. He was staring at her as if she were missing some ingredients herself. "What?"

"Yeah, I was talking about grown-up you, not high school you," he said. "From the list of suspects here with the explanations of why they might be miffed with you, it's clear you're a busybody. That's why you're in trouble. You just can't leave things alone."

"Busybody? You make me sound like I'm an old lady," she said.

"If the blue hair fits," he said. He glanced back down at the list. "You remind me of that old television show, the one where the old gal is always getting mixed up in investigations."

"Miss Marple?" she asked.

"Who?"

"You know, Agatha Christie," Mel said. "Greatest mystery writer of all time? Miss Marple is her amateur sleuth."

"You got the 'amateur' part right," he grunted. "No, I was thinking of the one with the old lady from Maine."

"Jessica Fletcher?" Mel asked.

He snapped his fingers and pointed at her. "That's the one. My grandmother loved that show."

"Well, Angela Lansbury is an icon of mine," Mel said. "So I'll let the comparison to a woman almost three times my age slide. This time."

"Whatever." He turned back to his laptop.

His fingers were clicking away and Mel wondered what he was discovering about the various people she had been tangled up with—in a crime-solving way—in the past. She wanted to ask him but she didn't want to listen to any more of his opinions about her character.

They worked in silence for a while, as Mel added her ingredients to her industrial Hobart mixer, until she couldn't take it anymore.

"So, any leads?" she asked. She tried to sound casual but Dwight was not having it.

"When I get a lead, dollface, you'll know it," he said.

Mel frowned. "Don't call me 'dollface.'"

"Why not?"

"Because it's demeaning," she said.

"How? It means you're cute." He looked thoroughly exasperated.

"Does it?" she asked. "Does it really?"

"What's that supposed to mean?" he asked.

"It means that you use compliments as a weapon," she said. She flipped on the mixer, filling the kitchen with the sound of its whir.

"What?!" Dwight cried, impressively louder than the Hobart.

"You didn't want to answer my question," Mel said. "So you complimented me, thinking you'd distract me from my purpose."

Dwight dug a hand into his close-cropped hair. "That makes absolutely no sense."

"Yes, it does."

"Only to a woman," he muttered.

Mel gasped. "What's that supposed to mean?"

"It means, *dollface*, that when I say something, I mean it. If I say I'll let you know when I find something, then I'll let you know," he said. "I stand my ground. *Dollface* is legit a compliment."

"Hmm." Mel frowned.

He mimicked her expression and asked, "Why are you so suspicious?"

"Because you've never complimented me before," she said.

"I never thought you were cute before," he said. "But now you're married."

"You find married women attractive?" Mel asked. This was an alarming complication that she absolutely did not need.

"Nah, I find them safe and uncomplicated." He grinned. "You can pay a married lady a compliment and she doesn't get all clingy and weird. In fact, she's so happy to have someone notice her, she's likely to fix a poor old bachelor a meal in return."

"Married or not, I have never been clingy or weird," Mel said.

Dwight stared at her. Hard.

"Okay, maybe I was a little weird in high school," she said. He kept staring. "All right, a lot weird, but you were mean."

"Agreed, and for that I *am* sorry," he said.

Dwight Pickard was apologizing and complimenting her. Mercury had to be in retrograde or something because this was *not* normal.

"Wait, so if you only hand out compliments to married women because they're safe, then does it even count?" she asked.

"Of course it does," he said. "I wouldn't say it if I didn't mean it."

"All right," Mel said. "Then thank you but do I have to be *dollface*? Can't I be *hottie* or *gorgeous*?"

"Reaching a little high there, Cooper," he said. "Excuse me, DeLaura."

"Fine . . . stud muffin," she replied.

Dwight's eyes went wide, his mouth opened, and he made a choking sound. Mel couldn't keep in the belly laugh that busted out of her at his expression. To his credit, he laughed, too.

Just then, the swinging door opened and Ray strode into the kitchen.

He glanced between the two of them. "What's going on here?"

"Nothing," Mel said. "Just goofing around."

Ray frowned. "Oh." He studied Dwight. "Why is he here?"

"Bodyguard," Dwight said, at the same time Mel said, "Cybersecurity."

"Bodyguard?" Ray asked. He looked offended. "That's what I'm here for."

"Excuse me?" Mel asked.

"Yeah, that's right," Ray said. "I stopped by Angie's this morning, and she told me what was happening. She's pretty upset that she can't come into the bakery, so I put her mind at ease by telling her I'd come over and protect you."

Dwight snorted and Mel saw Ray's eyes narrow. She left the mixer and impulsively hugged Ray, distracting him.

"That's so nice of you," she said. "But I really think it's unnecessary. I don't need a bodyguard."

"Yes, you do," the men said together.

Mel opened her mouth to argue but knew that this was a losing argument as far as these two were concerned and she had better things to do with her time, namely bake these cupcakes and then head next door and talk to Naomi to see if she'd remembered anything else from last night.

"Okay, fine," she said. "You do you but try not to get in the way."

"Cool," Ray said. He glanced at Dwight. "You can go. I've got this."

"No."

"What do you mean, 'no'?"

Ray planted his hands on his hips as if he couldn't believe the audacity. Mel tucked her smile in, not wanting to add to his outrage.

"I'm doing more than just being a bodyguard," Dwight said. He shot a glance at Mel. "Although, that is my main purpose."

"Yeah? What else are you doing? Baking?" Ray waved his hand at Dwight's apron.

"No, I'm doing an information deep dive on all of the people Mel has had 'issues' with," he said. "I'm trying to figure out who they are and where they are and whether they could have been responsible for last night's shooting."

"Oh." Ray looked at the laptop with distaste. "Well . . . that's . . . yeah."

Mel couldn't stand to see Ray feeling so displaced. She decided to put him out of his misery. "Ray, could you do me a favor and run upstairs and check on Oz? He hurt his ankle pretty badly last night and I didn't see him leave for work this morning. I'd go but—" She gestured to the ingredients all around her and the whirring machine.

Ray perked up. "Yeah, I could do that."

"Thanks," she said.

Ray disappeared and as soon as the door shut behind him, Dwight said, "Oz isn't going to thank you for that."

Mel shrugged. "Ray will keep Oz from brooding about his ankle and visiting Oz gives Ray something to do. Win-win."

"Hmm," Dwight hummed. "Not sure Oz would see it that way."

Mel ignored him and got to work baking her cupcakes. She was just piping the cream cheese frosting on top when Ray reappeared.

"The kid is good," he said. He sat down next to Dwight and before Mel could slap his hand away, he'd grabbed one of the newly frosted cupcakes. He leaned over Dwight's shoulder, getting crumbs on his keyboard. "What'd you find?"

Dwight brushed off his shoulder and his keyboard. "Do you mind?"

"No, that's why I asked," Ray said.

"That's not what I meant. Keep your crumbs to yourself, DeLaura."

Mel hefted a tray full of Hummingbird Cupcakes onto her shoulder and took them to the walk-in cooler. She was going to let the boys work this out for themselves.

She slid the tray onto the rolling cart with the other cupcakes she'd baked, then she rolled the entire cart back into the kitchen.

"I just think if we put our brains together—" Ray said but Dwight interrupted him.

"You mean my brain and your half brain?" Dwight asked.

"Hey!" Ray sputtered.

"I am not partnering with you, DeLaura. I am a solo unit. I operate alone."

"Because you don't have any friends?"

"No, because I like it that way."

"Sure you do."

They were glaring at each other and neither of them glanced up to see Mel wheel the cart out front. She pushed through the swinging door and parked the rolling cart next to the large display case. Marty was serving a customer sitting in a booth at the far end of the bakery, so she took the opportunity to box a couple of cupcakes to bring next door.

She'd be gone only a second. No one needed to know. Especially because if they knew she was popping in next door, they'd insist on going with her and Mel suspected they would make Naomi, who was still new to the area, skittish with their overabundance of personality.

She timed her exit just as a customer was entering so that when Marty glanced up, he'd see the customer and believe that was the reason the bells tied to the door handle were jangling. Mel would have patted herself on the back but she had places to go and people to see. Besides, what the boys didn't know wouldn't hurt them, right? Right.

Five

Mel dashed down the sidewalk and pulled on the handle of Naomi's Natural Soap. Immediately she was dipped in a honeypot of delicious scents. Vanilla. Bergamot. Blood orange. Sandalwood. Amber. She inhaled deeply, letting it fill her up.

"Hi, Mel!" Naomi greeted her from behind the counter in the section of the shop where she actually made the soap. Naomi was pouring a fresh batch into a large plastic rectangle while several customers perused the shop's offerings.

It was a genius setup. The shop was divided by a counter behind which Naomi crafted the cold-pressed soap. On the customer side, there were artistically arranged display cases made out of wooden barrels and crates, showcasing her paper-wrapped soaps, which were tied with twine and dried flowers. Truly, the aesthetic in here was off the charts.

"Hi, Naomi," Mel said. "I just popped in for a quick chat and I brought you some cupcakes."

"Ooh, thank you. Give me a second and I'll be right with you," Naomi said. "I have to pour while the pouring is good."

"Take your time."

Mel rested against the counter and watched her neighbor work. Using several plastic bottles, Naomi squirted circles of deep green and dusty purple onto the pale, sky blue mixture that was already in the rectangular mold. The process was very soothing, Mel thought, not as much as piping buttercream onto cupcakes but darn close.

Naomi used a long glass rod to then mix the new colors on top of the old, making cool waves and patterns of color. She pulled the glass rod through the mixture one way and then another. It looked like exotic feathers of green and purple on top of the pale blue. Lovely.

When she was satisfied, Naomi put the mold on a shelf on the wall. Mel noted there were several others there as well.

"May the saponification process begin," she said.

Mel raised her eyebrows in inquiry.

"That's the fancy way of saying *making soap*. If all goes well, in two to three days it'll be a solid mass of pine-and-juniper-berry-infused man soap." Naomi grinned. She wiped her fingers on her apron and held out her hands to Mel.

"It seems complicated," Mel said as she handed over the cupcakes.

"No more than baking cupcakes." Naomi lifted the lid

on the box and inhaled. "My lunch just got so much better."

"Hummingbird Cupcakes," Mel said.

"Yum." Naomi turned and put the cupcakes on her worktable. "That reminds me. Your bakery inspired me a few nights ago." She crossed over to a table with a stack of already-cut soaps, wrapped in brown paper, tied with twine, and decorated with a dried vanilla bean. She picked up the unwrapped brown and white square of soap that sat on top on display and handed it to Mel. "My version of the classic chocolate cupcake with vanilla icing."

Mel lifted the bar to her nose and smelled it. The complementary scents of chocolate and vanilla filled her nostrils and she groaned as she handed it back. "That smells amazing."

"Like a cupcake," Naomi agreed. She picked up a few of the already-wrapped bars and handed them to Mel. "Take these to share with your staff."

"I'll do better than that," Mel said. "I'll put them on display with a sign saying where to get them."

"Really?" Naomi asked. "Wow, that'd be great. Thanks, and I'll credit Fairy Tale Cupcakes for inspiring that soap."

Mel grinned. "I am so glad you bought the shop next door."

"Me, too," Naomi said. "I can only hope I am as successful as you. Right now, it's just me and my part-time assistant, Pam." She glanced at the cashier counter and Mel followed her gaze. There was a middle-aged woman wearing an apron just like Naomi's. She looked to be in her fifties with her short brown hair just showing some silver and a pair of reading glasses perched on her nose.

"She's my neighbor," Naomi said. "She doesn't need the money but wanted to get out of the house a few days per week. She told me she'd pay me to be here just to get away from her newly retired husband."

Mel laughed. "Yeah, I've got an employee like that. Good workers."

"The best," Naomi agreed. She lifted a section of the counter and walked through to join Mel on the customer side. She tipped her head toward the corner of the room and Mel followed her.

"Let's talk over there, okay?" Naomi asked. She kept her voice low so that the browsing customers wouldn't hear her.

Mel noticed that the people in the shop who'd been watching Naomi work had wandered off to examine her soap displays. Mel wondered if it boosted Naomi's sales to have people witness the process. Maybe she should open up her kitchen to public viewing. She tried to imagine piping frosting while people watched and shook her head. That was a no. Best to leave some mystery to the fairy tale.

"Are you all right?" Naomi asked. She put her hand on Mel's forearm and gave it a gentle squeeze. "The police told me someone shot at you last night. Is that true?"

"Yeah," Mel said. She forced a smile. "Luckily, they missed."

Naomi met her gaze and Mel noticed that Naomi was almost the same height as her, with a lean build, again like Mel, and wore her light brown hair in a short, spiky cut. Maybe this was why Mel felt such a kinship with the soap maker—they were a type.

"I had no idea this neighborhood was so dangerous,"

Naomi said. "I sunk everything I have into this shop and even took out a loan." She lowered her voice to a whisper. "Do you think the incident will have an impact on our business?"

"No," Mel said. She shook her head. "Bad stuff has happened here before and it's never turned off the tourists or the locals who flock to Old Town. We'll be fine."

Naomi looked so relieved, that Mel knew she had said the right thing even if she wasn't entirely certain of anything. Still, she felt it was always better to have a positive outlook.

"About last night," Mel said. "I know the police already asked you but I just thought maybe you might have remembered something since then. Are you sure you didn't see or hear anything weird?"

"Nothing. I really thought it was just a car backfiring," Naomi said regretfully. "And I'm so sorry about that. If I'd known you were in danger, I would have called the police myself or, I don't know, thrown some soap at the guy." She flexed her arm. "I'm stronger than I look."

Mel grinned. "I appreciate the thought but I'm glad you didn't get caught in the cross fire."

"Naomi, do we have any more lemon-scented soap?" Pam called from across the shop.

"Sure, I'll be right there," Naomi said. She pushed off the counter and gave Mel a chagrined look. "I'm sorry I can't be of more help."

"Don't worry about it," Mel said. "But if you think of anything—"

"I'll let you know right away," Naomi promised. "Anything to catch the person."

"Thanks," Mel said.

She left the shop and turned to walk back to the bakery. Standing on the patio out front were Marty, Dwight, and Ray and they looked upset. *Uh-oh.*

"That was not cool, boss," Marty said.

"Yeah, what he said," Dwight agreed.

Mel glanced between them. Sure, now they were getting along.

"What? I just went next door to bring Naomi a cupcake," she said. "I thought she might be worried about me and she was."

"You should have told me," Dwight said. "I'd have come with you."

"You were busy," Mel said. "Besides, I wanted to see if she remembered anything from last night that she forgot about when she talked to the police and I didn't think a crowd would help her remember."

"Still not cool. Besides, if she had, she should call Uncle Stan," Ray said.

Mel rolled her eyes. If they were going to get all persnickety about it, she had nothing more to say. She waved her hands at them in a shooing gesture. "Well, nothing happened, and I'm back now, so let's get back to work."

Dwight nodded. "That's fine but we'll be working from your house for the rest of the day."

"What?"

"Uncle Stan's orders," Dwight said. "He said if you started to insinuate yourself into the investigation, I was to take you home where you could do no harm and wouldn't get hurt."

"But I have more cupcakes to bake," Mel said.

"I called Oz," Marty said. "He's off today and said he'd come in and cover for you."

"But his ankle—"

"He said he was fine to cook," Marty interrupted her.

"But you can't work the counter alone," Mel said. "We get really busy and Madison doesn't come in today—"

"I'll stay and help," Ray offered.

Mel glanced at Marty in alarm, but he said, "Don't worry, he'll wear an apron, and I won't let him eat all of the stock."

"This is so uncool," Mel said.

Dwight nodded as he opened the front door and gestured for her to lead the way in. "Stan said you'd say that and that when you did, I was to call Joe, tell him the situation, and get his input."

Mel stopped walking and turned to stare at Dwight. "You'd tell on me?"

"One hundred percent," he said.

"What happened to 'snitches get stitches'?" she asked. "Wasn't that your credo in high school?"

"We're not in high school anymore," he said.

"Pity." Mel spun back around and flounced to her office to grab her handbag.

She took out her phone and checked her text messages. There were three from Angie, starting with her unhappiness at not being able to come into the bakery, expressing how bored she was, and ending with she'd meet Mel at her house in a few minutes.

Mel glanced up from her phone and saw Marty watching her. She had no doubt he was the one who'd let Angie know what was happening.

"At least you'll have a buddy in lockdown," he said. He gave her a sympathetic look.

"Thanks, Marty," she said. She gave him a hug and he patted her back.

"Don't get all emotional now," he said. "They'll catch the lunatic who shot at you and you'll be back in your kitchen in no time."

"I hope you're right," she said. She glanced at Dwight, who had packed up his laptop and was waiting. "All right, let's go."

It was a short drive to Mel's house and when they arrived Angie was already there, making grilled cheese sandwiches, while Emari bounced in her entertainment center.

Angie hugged Mel tight and then stepped back and frowned. "Why didn't you call me last night? The first I heard about the shooting was from Tate this morning when he said I couldn't go into the bakery."

"Sorry," Mel said. "It was a bit chaotic, plus if you were actually sleeping, I didn't want to wake you up."

"You can always wake me up," Angie said. "*Always.*"

"Okay," Mel said. She nodded her head and smiled. She should have known Angie would react that way. Then she frowned. "Should you be here though? I mean, if the shooter is gunning for me, aren't you putting yourself and Emari in danger?"

"No." Angie returned to the stove and waved her spatula at the window. "I can't be safer anywhere than here."

"Because of me, right?" Dwight's chest puffed up with pride.

"Hi, Dwight," Angie said. She had warmed up to him over the past year but he wasn't in her inner circle just yet. Angie had a long memory. "And, while I appreciate you being here, no, you're just the last line of defense."

Mel and Dwight exchanged a look. "What do you mean?" Mel asked.

"Did you not notice the mail truck parked in front of your house?" Angie asked.

Mel crossed the room and glanced out front. Sure enough, there was a mail truck with what appeared to be a flat tire. The mailman was sitting in the truck with his feet up on the dash, looking as if he was waiting for a tow.

"Yeah, so?" Mel asked.

"And the telephone repair company just happens to be working on the line that runs along the alley behind the house."

Mel crossed to the kitchen window and saw a utility truck with two guys in orange vests, parked just outside her back wall.

"Cops?" Dwight asked.

"Private security," Angie said. "Tate and Joe cooked it up last night, preparing for when you got sent home from work today."

Dwight burst out laughing while Mel made a puckered face as if she'd just bitten into a lime. "Seriously? Did they really think I couldn't handle a whole day at work?"

Angie flipped the grilled cheese sandwiches onto a serving plate. "Sandwiches?"

Mel stared at her. "Refusing to answer is answer enough."

"How about some potato chips?"

"Fine," Mel said. She glanced at Dwight. "Iced tea?"

"Yes, please."

Mel poured three glasses and they took their seats at the kitchen table. Angie waved and cooed at the baby, who drooled onto her pink bib, which read *Daddy's Girl*, in response. Then she clapped and chortled, seeming happy despite the tooth that was pushing through her lower gums.

"Sweet baby," Dwight said. Angie looked at him in pleased surprise and he added, "Must take after her dad."

"Ha-ha," Angie said. She threw a potato chip at him, which he caught and ate. Then she added, "She totally does."

The two exchanged a smile. Mel had heard people say that babies were magical. She glanced at Emari and thought it made perfect sense. There was a purity of spirit in that fine-haired, sixteen-pound bundle of joy that could not be denied.

They were just finishing up when Mel's and Angie's phones chimed at the same time. They exchanged a glance and reached for their phones. It was a text message from Tate.

Emergency meeting tonight for the members of the Old Town Small Business Association in regards to the shooting. I think we need to be there, Angie read.

Mel nodded. "I think he's right."

"I'm available," Dwight said.

Mel glanced at him with one eyebrow raised.

"Don't even think you're going alone," he said. "In fact, I'd bet money that you're going to have an entire DeLaura entourage surrounding you."

"Because that won't make things awkward," Mel said. She turned to Angie. "We can rein in the brothers, right?"

Angie bit her lip. "Maybe?"

Or maybe not, Mel thought as she strode into the courtyard of Los Olivos restaurant, flanked by her squad of DeLaura men and associates. Walking between Tate and Joe, Mel felt they were muscle enough, but no. The entourage included Marty, Oz, Ray, Paulie, Al, and Tony. The only brothers not present were Dom and Sal and that was because they were out of town. Joe had given Dwight the night off, feeling it was more important for him to run down the remaining names on his list.

Mel had spent her teen years watching as Angie was doted on and infuriated by her seven older brothers. Having just one brother, Charlie, Mel had often wondered what it would be like to have a built-in squad. Now she knew, and as Al and Paulie tussled over the mint bowl at the hostess station, Mel could see why Angie was occasionally cranky with her siblings. They were—to put it mildly—a bit much.

"Let's grab a table against the wall, facing the door," Ray said. He was dressed in black, per usual, and his hair had been slicked back from his forehead in the standard tough-guy hairdo.

Mel turned to Joe. "Someone spent his formative years watching *The Sopranos*, didn't he?"

Joe laughed and nodded. "Among other things. 'As far back as I can remember, I always wanted to be a gangster.'"

"*Goodfellas*." Mel and Tate identified the movie quote together and exchanged a fist bump.

"Was Angie okay with staying home?" Mel asked.

"No," Tate said. "But her life revolves around nursing Emari, plus she fell asleep. I expect I'll hear about it when I get home."

"Is she all right by herself?" Mel asked.

"She's not by herself," Tate said. He jerked his chin at Joe. "Your hubby has people watching the house."

Mel turned to Joe, who paused at the table Ray had chosen for them and pulled her chair out for her. "Thanks, I would have worried."

Joe shrugged. "I have people watching all of our houses, including Marty's, your mom's, and Oz's apartment above the bakery. Until we know who the shooter is and why they went after you, we take no chances."

Mel felt her stomach clench. She hated that everyone was potentially at risk and they didn't know why. She refused to believe that it was someone coming after her or one of her staff for revenge. Dwight had impressively tracked down every person who had been in conflict with the bakery over the years and there were a few who were suspicious and at large, but Mel just couldn't see it. The bigger task was tracking down the family and friends of those people, but Dwight was confident it wouldn't take him that long.

Joe had just scratched the surface of criminals that he'd put away over the years. It would take days, possibly weeks, to track down every person he had prosecuted successfully. Mel knew this was his worst nightmare, thinking that his job was putting her at risk. She didn't have the heart to tell him she hoped it was his job instead of something she'd done over the years. Despite the fact that he was her husband and best friend, she knew better than to share this feeling as she was quite certain he did not feel the same.

As soon as they were all seated at the table, Ray ordered several pitchers of margaritas and chips and salsa from their waitress. Tony gave him a look but Ray shrugged and said, "I'm hungry."

"Do you really think sucking down margaritas when there's a shooter on the loose is the best strategy?" Tony asked.

"Don't be such a buzzkill," Ray said. "Besides, I'm planning on sopping up those margs with the carne asada plate."

"Now you're talking," Tony said. "Let's make it two."

The waitress took everyone's orders. Mel wasn't hungry, so she chose to split a sampler plate with Joe. She was too preoccupied with scanning the courtyard to care much about food, which never happened. She saw several of the small-business owners that she knew. Mick Donnelly, who owned the tattoo parlor down the street, was sitting with Millie Carpenter, whose petite plant shop specialized in succulents.

Mel waved at them, and Mick smiled and waved back. Millie, however, frowned at her. Mel blinked. She and Millie had always gotten along and she wondered what she could have done that made the delicate woman glare at her.

"Good evening, everyone." John Billings stood at the far end of the dining area. He was the president of the Old Town Small Business Association, primarily because he owned a landmark steak house along with several other businesses in the area. If businesses were pie, John had a slice of all of them. He was a fixture in Old Town and was usually seen walking around the district in cowboy boots and a big Stetson, with his signature handlebar mustache covering the lower half of his face. He was a big man with a low voice and it boomed out across the courtyard, capturing everyone's attention. The conversations, which had been loud, dimmed as the crowd turned to face him.

"Thank you all for coming on such short notice," he said. He spoke slowly, his voice a deep drawl. "We have a situation in Old Town that we all need to be aware of to make certain it isn't the start of a problem."

Mel saw most of the gathering nod in agreement. She glanced around her table and noticed that the men here, too, were all nodding as well. This was why John was the president. He had a way of bringing people together. Mel wasn't sure if it was the mustache or the deep voice but he had a very Sam Elliott vibe that everyone seemed to respect.

"I think by now you're all aware that there was a shooting behind Fairy Tale Cupcakes bakery last night," he said. He cringed a little bit when he said the name and Mel wished Angie were here to appreciate the pain it caused him to say something so girlie. John glanced over at their table and nodded at Mel. "I think I speak on behalf of everyone here when I say I'm glad you're all right, Mel."

"Thanks," she said. Her voice was drowned out, however, by Nikki Guthrie from across the room.

"John! Yoo-hoo, John!" Nikki stood and waved her hand to get his attention. When he turned toward her, she tossed her hair in a practiced move and said, "I'd like to say something."

John shrugged. "Okay."

Nikki tugged on the lapels of her blue blazer as if

she'd be taken more seriously if it sat just so on her person. She owned a small jewelry store off Marshall Way and was often seen on the sidewalk in front of her store, chatting up the tourists and inviting them into her shop. Angie always referred to her as the spider in her web.

She was a faux blonde, artificially curvy, and middle-aged but leaving claw marks on her thirties with a face that had a plastic sheen to it from too much filler. In other words, she was the poster model for the privileged Scottsdale woman-about-town.

Mel frowned. She'd had a run-in or two with Nikki over the years and each time it had been unpleasant. Nikki seemed to feel that a cupcake bakery was not of the same caliber of business as a jewelry store. She wondered what Nikki had to say to the group and even though Mel suspected it would be something mean, she was completely unprepared for the bomb Nikki dropped.

"As a long-standing member of the Old Town Small Business Association, I move that Fairy Tale Cupcakes bakery be closed," Nikki said.

Six

Audible gasps, one of which came from Marty, filled the courtyard.

"The nerve!" he cried. Oz shushed him.

Undaunted by the shocked response, Nikki pressed on. "That bakery has been nothing but trouble since the day it opened. How many times has someone been murdered in and around that place? I'm telling you, it's cursed. Get rid of her"—Nikki paused to point a bony acrylic-tipped finger at Mel, before she concluded—"and the violence will go away."

"Now wait just a minute," Marty yelled as he popped up from his seat. Oz wrapped a hand around Marty's elbow and tugged him back down.

"Take it easy," Oz said. "You don't want to lose your temper and prove her point, do you?"

"No," Marty muttered. He sounded as if he had to think about it and still wasn't sure.

John Billings turned to look at Mel. He looked dismayed, as if he clearly hadn't expected a reaction like that. That made two of them, Mel thought.

Tate, who was the schmoozer of the bakery, stood. He was in a dress shirt and slacks. He oozed financial genius out of every pore and Mel knew he was the perfect person to take Nikki on.

"I think that's an oversimplification of the current situation, don't you agree, John?"

John paused to stroke his mustache. Finally, he nodded. He turned back to Nikki and said, "I don't think we can demand that the bakery close when we have no idea why the shooter was in the alley to begin with. We don't know if he was planning to attack Mel or if she just happened to be at the wrong place at the wrong time."

"Oh, I see," Nikki said. She waved a dismissive hand at him. "You're afraid of her."

John frowned. He opened his mouth to protest but she forged on.

Nikki waved her arm at their table. "You're afraid of her entourage."

Mel wasn't positive but she thought she detected a note of jealousy in Nikki's voice.

"Well, who wouldn't be?" John asked. He winked, letting everyone know he was kidding. "I think we can table this discussion for now and get back to the agenda. I think it's important that we all make an effort to pay attention to our surroundings, the buddy system should always be used when you lock up your shops, and if anyone sees anything suspicious they should report it to the police immediately."

"Idiot," Nikki muttered just loud enough for everyone to hear. She sounded annoyed and Mel figured she was angry that John hadn't taken action about her suggestion to close down the bakery immediately.

John ignored her and kept on going. "Now, we have a member of the Scottsdale PD here to give us a few pointers and tips for spotting trouble. Detective, can you come up here?"

Mel followed the direction of John's gaze and saw a woman with her back to them at the bar. She lifted her pint and drained what remained in one swallow, then she swiveled around to face them. It was Uncle Stan's partner, Tara Martinez.

Short, curvy, and packed with attitude, she strode across the room to stand next to John. She was dressed in her off-duty clothes, which looked just like her work clothes: khaki trousers, a white dress shirt, and a blue blazer. When she walked, the badge clipped to her belt was visible.

"That's my girl," Ray said. Not born with a whisper, his voice carried across the room and Tara sent him a look that would have frozen a lesser man into a block of ice. Not Ray. He just grinned at her and she shook her head, as if ignoring him might make him go away.

"Good evening," she said. She glanced around the room. "I want to assure you that the Scottsdale Police Department is taking the event from last night very seriously."

"Do you have any suspects?" Clint Carlisle asked. He owned an exotic pet store. Given that it featured an enormous yellow boa constrictor, Mel had never been in his shop nor did she think he had anything to fear from a random gunman in town. Who in their right mind would try to rob his shop?

"Not at this time," Tara said. She paused and added, "But we do have several leads."

Mel wondered if their main lead was the car Oz saw and the numbers off the plate that he'd remembered. Tara didn't say.

"And what do you think about closing the bakery?" Nikki asked.

Tara's eyebrows rose in displeasure. She didn't like being interrupted repeatedly. She ignored Nikki and continued speaking as if the jewelry store owner weren't there.

"I want to reiterate what Mr. Billings said. There is to be no vigilantism in Old Town. With the influx of spring tourists, it could have disastrous consequences." She swept the room with a hard stare. "You are not to try and find the culprit yourselves. If you see or hear anything that causes you concern, you are to call the police immediately."

She reached into her pocket and held up a stack of business cards. "I am leaving my cards with John to give to anyone who wants one. It is my direct line. Call me anytime day or night if you have any suspicions."

In the pause Tara took to catch her breath, Nikki stood up. She glared at Mel and her table. "You didn't answer my question. What do you think about closing the bakery?

Don't you think if they are the target that it would be better for everyone if they shut down?"

"What is her damage?" Joe whispered to Mel. "She is a badger, completely obsessed with shutting you guys down."

"I have no idea," Mel said. "She's never liked me but this is all-new levels of hostility." She glanced at Tate. "Do you know what her problem with us is?"

Tate winced and put his hand on the back of his neck, looking distinctly uncomfortable. "It could be that when we bought the building for the bakery, we put an end to her bid for leasing the property."

"Oh." Mel nodded. "So, it's a grudge."

"Looks like it," he said.

"Well, it's not like she can do anything other than complain," Joe said.

"Yeah," Al agreed. "It's just noise."

The brothers all seemed satisfied with this, but Mel wasn't so sure. Grudges could be powerful things.

"I have started a petition," Nikki announced. She held up a sheaf of papers and waved them in the air. "I am gathering signatures demanding that for the safety and well-being of the business owners, residents, and tourists of Old Town, Fairy Tale Cupcakes be shut down."

The courtyard erupted into yelling, mostly Mel's table, and much to her horror there was a random smattering of applause. Clearly, some of the businesses supported Nikki. Mel felt betrayed on a molecular level.

"You just try it!" Marty yelled. He hopped up from his chair and made to charge Nikki. Thankfully, Oz and Al were right behind him and scooped him up by the arms, hauling him outside before he reached her.

Tony studied the woman as if looking for her weak spots. Given that Tony was the mysterious high-tech De-Laura, Mel would have felt sorry for Nikki, but she was trying to shut them down, so no.

Mick Donnelly stood up. He held his hands out in a calm-down gesture. Because he was big and broad and loaded with tattoos, piercings, and a few metal implants, he looked like something that had crawled out of a hell mouth and no one wanted to tangle with him.

"Why would you do this, Nikki?" he asked. "Old Town businesses are family. We look out for each other."

"Because that bakery has been a cancer in our neighborhood for too long," Nikki said. "You can fool yourself that they contribute to the community but they don't. And the only way to deal with cancer is to cut it out before it spreads."

"That's it," Tate said. He stood up, threw his napkin down, and planted his hands on his hips. "I'm sorry but you are so far off base, you're not even in the stadium."

Nikki stuck her chin up in the air. "No, I'm not. Your bakery is a detriment to Old Town."

"Really?" Tate snapped. "Because we sell over one hundred and fifty thousand cupcakes per year. Do you have any idea how much foot traffic that brings into Old Town?"

Nikki blinked. Mel felt a surge of satisfaction as she watched Tate gear up for a full-on financial-facts-and-figures takedown.

"A lot," Tate snapped. "You want to kick us out, Nikki? Think of how many people buy a cupcake and wander through the community, window-shopping. You really want to lose that business?"

Nikki visibly bristled. She clearly did not like being called to account.

"Ooooh," she mocked him. "I'm so glad you're soooo successful. I call BS on your theory. No one is going to buy a four-dollar cupcake and then come and spend real money in my jewelry store. People who buy overpriced pastries don't appreciate the finer things."

"Actually, I'd argue that they do," Tony said. "The demographic for who can afford a high-end cupcake is exactly who would buy handmade artisan jewelry, and the people who consider a four-dollar cupcake a treat, well, they would never happen across your store unless, as Tate pointed out, they were to wander by while enjoying their cupcake. How many customers have you gained, who never would have found you, if it weren't for those high-end pastries?"

"Shut up!" Nikki snapped. "No one asked you and besides, you don't even own a business here." She turned to the other business owners, who now looked extremely uncomfortable, and demanded, "Sign the petition. Sign it and we'll get rid of the bad element in Old Town once and for all. With enough signatures, I plan to go to the mayor and the city council, requesting that Fairy Tale Cupcakes be shut down—permanently."

"I really want to slap her," Mel whispered to Joe.

"You aren't alone there," he said. "Best not to, however."

71

"I suppose," she agreed.

"If you're all finished?" Tara asked. She looked peeved. "Contrary to what Ms. Guthrie here says, there is no reason to suspect that the shooting has anything to do with the bakery. We have no way of knowing if the shooter was aiming for the staff of the bakery or if the person who was shot at just happened to step out of their establishment at the wrong time."

She didn't say Mel's name but everyone looked at her anyway. Her face grew warm and she felt intensely uncomfortable under their scrutiny. Instead of hiding under the table like she wanted to, however, she tipped her chin up and stared Nikki down. The jewelry store owner was the first to look away.

There was some grumbling among the other business owners and Mel hoped they took Tara's words to heart. Personally, given that Tara had never been overly fond of Mel, she was surprised the detective had defended her and the bakery as staunchly as she had.

Mel glanced around the room. She got a weird feeling in her gut when she looked at the faces of the people she'd considered her friends for so many years and saw that they were conflicted. *Conflicted!* As if they truly believed the bakery had brought the shooting to the neighborhood. Mel hated to think that any of the business owners thought the bakery was a bad influence in the district. No one met her gaze.

She chose to take it as a good sign, that everyone felt guilty for not defending the bakery, and hoped that Nikki's nasty insinuations were dusted and done.

"I'll sign," Brenda Jacobs said as she rose to her feet.

She sent a dirty look at their table as she walked over to Nikki.

Brenda owned a sandwich shop right in the heart of Old Town. She was young and hip with an arm full of tattoos and a wild mane of sky blue hair. Mel had always considered her an ally, plus she made a wicked pastrami on marble rye. She was stunned by the defection and more than a little hurt.

"That might be my fault," Tony said. He kept his voice low but when Mel glanced up she noticed that the eyeball daggers Brenda was sending their way were definitely aimed at Tony.

"Ah." Mel nodded. She glanced around the table and asked, "Any other DeLaura brother break some hearts in Old Town? Speak now so we know what we're dealing with."

All of the brothers, with the exception of Joe, glanced away. Al started to whistle. Mel rolled her eyes and looked at her husband. "The DeLaura family charm strikes again."

Joe shrugged, raised his hands in the air, and said, "Italian."

Mel watched as more and more business owners got in line to sign the petition. Could they really drive the bakery out of Scottsdale?

"No," Tate said as if reading her mind. "They can sign all the petitions they want but we own the building that the bakery is in, we've done nothing wrong, and there's no reason for them to want us gone other than sheer petty meanness."

Mel tried to take his words to heart but as she watched

Nikki passing out pens, she felt her insides shrivel up. She was really glad Angie wasn't here to see this. It would break her heart.

"I don't want you gone," Mick said. He left his table and joined theirs, taking Marty's vacated seat, and Mel noticed that Millie wasn't with him. She glanced back at the petition line and sure enough, there she was.

"Has everyone always felt this hostility toward the bakery?" she asked.

He shook his head. "I've never heard anyone bad-mouth you guys before, but then times have been tough and the bakery is amazingly successful. People get jealous."

Mel nodded. "I could understand that if we were all competing bakeries but we're not. I mean, my cupcakes are no threat to Nikki's jewelry or Millie's succulents."

"No, but you don't have to win over every single customer who comes into your shop like they do," he said. "They are surviving sale to sale."

"Much like the bakery when we first opened," Mel said.

"So, you know the struggle. Imagine if things had never improved."

"But you're ridiculously successful and they don't hate you," Mel said.

Mick paused as he poured himself a glass from the pitcher of margaritas. He lifted one pierced eyebrow at her. "They might," he said. "But if you were them would you ever admit it to me?"

She took in the whole package of tattoos and piercings and metal implants. "Fair point. But we've worked so hard to be successful. How can they begrudge us that?"

"Because in their minds, they have worked just as hard, which is why your success is so infuriating," he said. "They wonder, why you? Why were you successful instead of them?"

"Choice of product," Mel said. She pointed to Tate with her thumb. "And having a financial wizard as an investor."

"Yeah, they really hate you for that," he said. "Safety nets are very rare in small-business land."

"All this time, and I never knew how they felt," Mel said. She thought about it. When she'd first opened the shop, Nikki and Millie and the others now signing the petition were their regulars. As the years passed, and the bakery became more successful, she hadn't seen them as often. If she was honest with herself, she hadn't noticed their departure. She wondered what it said about her that she hadn't noticed. Nothing good.

Mel frowned. Joe, with a thoughtful expression, was listening to Mick while Tate spoke with the business owners who clustered around their table because they weren't signing the petition. At a glance, it appeared that the room was split fifty-fifty, but Tate was trying to boost their favorability.

"Do you think Nikki has been just waiting for something like this to happen so she could try and get the building?" Joe asked.

"I don't know," Mick said. "She probably just has it in her head that the bakery is so successful because of location and if she'd just gotten to lease the space before you bought it, maybe she'd be that successful, too."

"How far would she go to get possession of the building?" Tony asked. They all turned to look at him but he was regarding Mel with a considering gaze. "Is she the same height and build as the shooter?"

Mel turned and studied Nikki. Was she the same size? Mel tried to imagine the jewelry store owner standing in an alley, dressed all in black, and firing a gun at Mel. Just then Nikki met her gaze and the hatred was almost palpable. Yup, she could totally see it.

"It's hard to say," she said. "There was a lot of adrenaline flowing. I was up on a landing, it was dark, the person was dressed all in black . . . I don't know . . . No . . . Maybe?"

Tony nodded. "Close enough." He turned to Joe. "We need to find out what she drives and what the license plate is."

Joe nodded. He was already on his phone texting. "I'm putting Dwight on it right now."

Mel frowned at the people gathered around the petition. She really couldn't believe they were signing. She felt someone step up beside her and she turned to find Lyn Andres Anderson standing there. Lyn was one of Mel's favorite business owners in Old Town. She was an artist, a clay sculptor who had a small studio next door to Millie's succulent shop and resided in Old Town during the winter months. As soon as it got too hot, she headed back up to Canada.

Lyn was known for the head scarves she wore and today's was a fabulous deep purple with silver threads running through it. It accentuated her pretty green eyes, which at the moment were narrowed in concern as she glanced from Mel to Nikki and back.

"Why is she so mean?" Lyn asked. "I mean, where am I supposed to get my daily intake of carbs, fat, and sugar if they close down your bakery?"

That surprised a laugh out of Mel, which she suspected was Lyn's intention. She threw an arm around Lyn's shoulders and gave her a squeeze. "How are the kids?"

"They're teenagers," Lyn said. She pushed back the scarf she wore so that Mel could see her black and silver hair. "As you can see, it's getting more silver by the minute."

Mel laughed again.

"Seriously, though," Lyn said. Her gaze met Mel's and held it. "Are you okay?"

"I'm fine," Mel said. She hoped she sounded more confident than she felt. "I mean, we have no idea why anyone shot at me, and I still believe it was wrong place, wrong time, but I am confident that the police will figure it out."

"I'm sure you're right," Lyn said. "Just so you know, you're welcome to drop by the studio whenever you want to punch a block of clay if you need it."

"Thanks," Mel said. "I may just take you up on that."

"Do," Lyn said. She patted Mel's arm before heading to the exit. Nikki tried to flag her down but Lyn waved her off like an annoying mosquito. Mel made a mental note to bring the ceramicist some cupcakes tomorrow.

"They're hoping this shooting tanks your business," Tony said.

Mel frowned at him. He jerked a thumb toward the group across the courtyard and said, "I was eavesdropping."

"That's so mean of them. I would never enjoy watching any of them fail," Mel said.

"No, you wouldn't," Mick agreed. "You're not built that way. But our society loves to watch a person or business build itself up from nothing and then have the chair kicked right out from under them."

"So, they're enjoying our free fall?"

"So it would seem," he agreed.

"But you're not," she said.

"Well, no, because I'm a real friend."

Mel smiled at him, then gave him a quick hug. "Thanks, Mick."

He hugged her back. "I know it feels very personal but try not to take it that way. People struggle with the success of others. It's not right but they do."

"I don't know," Mel said. "Nikki really seems to enjoy the fact that I was almost shot. That smirk is going to be hard to forget."

"If the rumors are true, she won't be in business much longer," Mick said. "Her schadenfreude is coming from a very dark place." Ray gave him a questioning look and Mick explained, "It's a German word that means 'taking pleasure in the misery of others.'"

"Perhaps." Mel took a moment to take that in. "I'm trying to be sympathetic. It's a struggle."

"You're a better person than me," Joe said. "I can't get over the fact that she's trying to destroy your business in the wake of you almost being murdered. What sort of a person does that?"

"An angry one," Mick answered.

They all glanced back at Nikki and the line of business

78

owners at her table. She looked like a queen holding court. It was sickening.

Again, Mel tried to remember what the shooter had looked like but her memories of the incident were just a blur. It had been dark and the person had been in the shadows and dressed all in black. She had no idea if Nikki was the right height or weight to have been the one to shoot at her. What she did know was that she much preferred thinking it had been a stranger.

"Come on, let's get out of here," Tate said. "I need a cupcake or five."

"To the bakery!" Ray cried. He threw his arm around Tara and she gave him a look. "Or not."

"We're meeting my parents for dinner or did you forget?" she asked.

"Nope, didn't forget," Ray said. "Just got distracted by frosting."

Tara pursed her lips. "Acceptable."

It was dark when they left the meeting. Oz and Marty and Al were still outside. The other brothers begged off the comfort eating and it was just Mel, Joe, Tate, Oz, and Marty who walked through Old Town back to the bakery.

Once they left the toxic environment of the business meeting behind, Mel felt her shoulders drop. She couldn't take Nikki and her misguided attempt to harm the bakery to heart. She just had to scrape it off and hope that the shooter was caught, putting an end to all of this madness.

She was debating a lemon cupcake with raspberry buttercream versus a red velvet with cream cheese frosting—dilemma!—when Oz, who was in front of her, stopped short. Mel slammed into his back and was prevented from falling only because of Joe's quick reflexes.

"Oz, are you okay?" Mel asked.

"No." Oz shook his head. He pointed down the alley and they all looked in that direction. At the bottom of the stairs behind Naomi's soap shop was a body.

Seven

"No, no, no!" Mel cried. She skirted around Oz and broke into a run.

"Mel, wait!" Joe shouted as he dashed after her.

But she didn't slow down. She recognized Naomi from her short cropped hair and long, lanky build, even crumpled in a heap on the pavement.

Mel dropped to her knees beside the soap maker. Joe was next to her, already on the phone calling for an ambulance. Naomi's eyes were open and she had a hand pressed to her leg. It was covered in blood.

"Naomi, can you hear me?" Mel asked. "What happened?"

"Sh . . . shot," Naomi said. She shivered.

"Who shot you?" Mel asked.

"D-don't know. Didn't s-see them."

"She's going into shock," Tate said. He yanked his shirt over his head and wadded it into a ball. He pressed it onto the spot on Naomi's leg where she'd been pressing her hand.

"Naomi, stay with me," Mel said. She clutched the woman's hand. It was sticky with blood but her fingers were icy to the touch.

She could hear Joe talking but her concentration was solely on Naomi and trying to keep her with them. Mel leaned over her and ordered, "Naomi, look at me."

Naomi blinked. She appeared to have a hard time focusing.

"She's losing too much blood," Tate said. "She must have been shot near a major artery."

Marty's voice came from over their heads and it was a colorful litany of swear words. A tiny smile curved Naomi's lips.

In the distance, Mel could hear an ambulance wail. If they could just get her to hang on.

"Naomi, tell me about your process," Mel said. "I want to hear about how you make your soap. Start to finish."

Tate was putting his full weight on her leg. Naomi's hand was limp in Mel's. Mel felt her heart pound in a panicked staccato that they might lose Naomi before the EMTs arrived.

"Come on, Naomi," Mel said. "Talk to me."

Joe squeezed Mel's shoulder in reassurance.

Naomi licked her lips and said, "I don't want you to steal my trade secrets."

A surprised chuckle busted out of Mel. She glanced up and saw Marty and Oz, who were racing to the end of the alley to flag the ambulance down. They might just make it.

"Like I'm going to put soap in my cupcakes," Mel said. She wanted to see the usual sparkle in the other woman's eyes, which were squinched up in pain.

"It would bring . . . new meaning . . . to washing your mouth out with soap," Naomi quipped. She looked like she was about to laugh but instead she winced and let out a low moan. She started to pant as if she couldn't get enough air and she was shivering.

Mel exchanged a panicked look with Tate. He was sweating while pressing his shirt into her wound. The shirt was soaked through. Joe was still on the phone; he was describing Naomi's condition in a low voice as if she might overhear and be offended.

"Keep talking. We have to keep her with us," Tate said.

Mel glanced over his shoulder. She could see the flash of lights at the end of the alley. They only had to get Naomi to hang on for a few more minutes.

She hunkered down lower so she was in Naomi's line of sight. She was kneeling in the other woman's blood and the coppery smell with its particular tang hit her nose. She swallowed hard.

"So, tell me about the process," Mel said. "How do you make the soap?"

Naomi met her gaze and Mel saw the fear in the other woman's eyes. She knew it was bad. There was no pretending.

"They're almost here," Mel said. "Stay with me."

Naomi drew in a ragged breath. "You add water to the lye, slowly. Once it's dissolved, you move onto your oils. You have to heat up the coconut oil so it's a liquid and then you . . ." She let out a weak moan.

"Don't leave me hanging, Naomi, I'm in suspense here," Mel said. "Then what do you do?"

"You add your other oils, like sunflower, then you wait until it's one hundred degrees Fahrenheit before adding your lye water."

Her eyes rolled back into her head and Mel yelled, "Naomi!"

Naomi blinked and she was back . . . bareiy. She squinted at Mel. "I can't think . . . I can't hang on."

"Yes, you can," Mel said. "Think of your soap, think of your business, you have to—"

"Make way, coming through!" Marty yelled as he led the EMTs to Naomi.

Joe pulled Mel back and a medic took her spot. Tate relinquished his bloody shirt. Mel watched, her body rigid and her hands clenched into fists as the team began to work.

"I'm right here, Naomi," she said. She made sure she was in Naomi's line of sight. "Don't you worry. I'm not leaving you."

"Thank you," Naomi's voice was barely a whisper. "Can you call my husband, David? My phone is in my bag. He's listed under . . ." She paused to catch her breath. "He's listed as *David S*."

"Yes, absolutely," Mel said. She reached into Naomi's bag, which was on the ground beside her. With shaking fingers, she opened the contacts and chose David's name. She had no idea what to say.

"I can talk to him," Joe said. Mel gratefully handed him the phone.

Mel turned to the medic and asked, "Are you taking her to the hospital on Osborn?"

"Yup, as soon as she's stable."

Mel glanced at Joe to see that he'd heard. He nodded and wandered away from the group with Naomi's phone to his ear. Mel watched in gratitude as the medics went to work. In mere minutes, Naomi was tended and loaded onto a stretcher. Joe returned and handed Mel Naomi's phone and she put it in Naomi's shoulder bag and gave it to the medic as they loaded the stretcher into the back of the ambulance.

The medic following the stretcher being pushed by his two partners slowed as he passed by Tate, who was completely soaked in blood, and said, "Nice work. You may have saved her life."

With that, he slammed the door of the ambulance shut and hurried into the driver's seat. As the ambulance departed, a police car arrived. Mel recognized Salazar and Margolis and was relieved to see familiar faces. Behind them an unmarked car stopped and Uncle Stan climbed out. His expression was grim as he jogged toward them.

He didn't even wait until he was close but yelled down the alley, "What are you doing here, Mel? You're not supposed to be here."

Mel raised her hands in the air. "We had an emergency local business meeting."

"I know my partner was there, but you were supposed to be at home," he said. He turned to Tate. "Why did you let her go?"

"I didn't think anyone would try to shoot her in a crowd," Tate said. "And they didn't."

"No, instead they shot the woman who looks remarkably like Mel," Uncle Stan snapped.

Mel sucked in a breath. Was he saying that whoever shot Naomi had mistaken her for Mel? She felt sick to her stomach.

"You don't mean—" That was all she got out before Uncle Stan hauled her into a bear hug that squeezed the remaining breath out of her.

"Are you all right?" he asked. His voice was gruff.

"I'm fine, but Naomi—" Her throat got tight and her eyes watered up. Why was it she was always okay until someone asked how she was doing and then she fell apart? Her voice was wobbly when she added, "You think my neighbor Naomi was shot because of me."

Uncle Stan released her and held her by her upper arms. "I honestly don't know, but I don't like that you were shot at, she resembles you, and now she was shot, too."

"Do you think it's a stalker who likes a certain type?" Marty asked.

Uncle Stan patted his pocket, looking for an antacid pill. "I don't know. The whole world has gone crazy. Tell me what happened."

They all started talking at once. Uncle Stan popped the tablet in his mouth and ground it between his molars like it had done something to offend him. Then he held up his hands. "Whoa, whoa, whoa. One at a time. Joe, you start."

Joe slid his arm around Mel in support and she turned to him and asked, "Is her husband going to the hospital?"

"Yes, he's on his way to the emergency room," he said. He looked conflicted. "I didn't tell him exactly what had happened, just that there'd been an accident and she was on her way to the hospital. I didn't want to panic him as he sounded pretty upset."

Uncle Stan nodded. "That's fine. I'll have an officer intercept him and explain things in detail." He turned to Margolis and said, "Send someone."

She nodded.

Uncle Stan turned back to their group. "Now from the beginning."

"We walked back from the meeting at Los Olivos and were going to stop at the bakery for cupcakes. When we rounded the corner, Oz spotted Naomi. She was lying at the bottom of the staircase." Joe paused and then added, "It was clear from the blood loss that she'd been shot, so Tate tried to stop the bleeding, Mel talked to her to keep her conscious, I called an ambulance, while Oz and Marty waved the EMTs in."

"Anyone else have anything to add?" Uncle Stan asked.

They were all silent, absorbing the gravity of what had happened.

"That covers it," Tate said. He looked pale and shaky.

"Yeah," Mel said. "It all happened so fast. I didn't see anything except Naomi."

Uncle Stan turned to Salazar as Margolis was still on her phone. "You know what to do."

They nodded and stepped away from the group to plan out their canvas of the area.

"Come on," Uncle Stan said. "You two need to clean up."

Tate and Mel looked at each other. They were both covered in blood. Tate wobbled on his feet and Oz caught him under the arm.

"I got you, T," he said. "You can clean up at my place. I have some clothes you can wear."

Tate leaned hard against him. "Thanks. If I go home like this, it'll scare the daylights out of Angie."

They were all quiet. No one wanted that.

Marty hurried on ahead to unlock the bakery door, while Mel, Joe, and Uncle Stan followed. Oz helped Tate up the stairs to his place.

"We'll make some coffee," Mel called after them. A small smile and a nod was Tate's only response.

Once in the bakery, Mel disappeared into her office. She had a change of clothes in there that she kept around in case of the random baking catastrophe. She washed up in the staff bathroom and donned the clean shorts and T-shirt, bagging her blood-soaked outfit and dropping it on the floor to be dealt with later. She had no idea if she'd be able to save her clothes and she didn't much care. When she rejoined the others in the kitchen, the coffee was made and they were sitting at the table, looking shell-shocked and weary.

Uncle Stan wasn't there but Marty and Joe were. They also had a pile of cupcakes between them and Mel reached for a gluten-free grapefruit-flavored one, feeling like she needed the vitamin C boost. It was a rich citrus cake topped with a decadent chai buttercream. The first mouthful of sugary goodness leveled her anxiety right out.

Joe put his arm around her shoulders and hauled her up against his side. Mel slid her arm around his back, locking herself in. They didn't need to say anything. She knew what he was thinking. It could have been her. She took another bite of the cupcake.

The back door opened and Tate and Oz entered. Tate was wearing an overly large Eminem T-shirt with a pair of jeans that were too long and held up by a wide leather belt. Mel noticed that Oz was both taller and wider than Tate. When had that happened?

"Have a cupcake," Marty said. "It'll restore your mellow."

They didn't need to be told twice. Both Tate and Oz reached for a cupcake, biting into the confections as if they had medicinal properties, which honestly Mel thought they might.

"Well," Tate said. He'd finished his first cupcake and was pondering his second. "I suppose we need to talk about what happened."

"Should we wait for Uncle Stan?" Mel asked. "He probably has more information."

"Someone shot Naomi," Joe said. "Because they thought—"

He stopped speaking as if he couldn't bear to finish the sentence.

No one spoke. Mel glanced around the table. Oz, Marty, Tate, and Joe all wore matching expressions of distress. Mel knew what they were thinking. She also knew that they thought if they didn't say it then it wouldn't be true. But there was no avoiding it.

"Because they thought she was me," Mel said.

One by one they glanced at her. Still, they didn't speak. But Joe nodded. He dropped the cupcake he'd been about to eat.

"You can't be here," he said. "In fact, I don't think you should be at home, either."

Mel sighed. "If I can't be at work and I can't be at home, where do you suggest I go?"

"I hear Sweden's nice this time of year," Marty said.

Mel smiled. No one else did. She gave them all a stern look. "I am not going to Sweden."

"Italy?" Joe offered.

Mel stared at him.

"I'm sorry, cupcake," he said. "I just don't think it's safe for you here. Maybe Uncle Stan can hook you up with a safe house or something."

"Safe house?" Mel repeated. "Are you listening to yourself?"

"More importantly, are you listening to him?" Marty asked. He clapped a hand to his bald head in a gesture of complete exasperation. "You. Aren't. Safe. Here."

"You don't know that," Mel protested. "Just because someone shot at me and then actually shot Naomi doesn't mean that I'm in danger. It could still be a random burglar."

"Intent on stealing cupcakes or soap?" Tate asked. His voice was quiet. His face creased with worry. "Mel, you're my best friend. I don't think I could bear it if anything happened to you, especially if it's because we weren't cautious enough."

Mel wanted to argue. She did. But she knew that if the situation was reversed and if any of these guys were in danger, she'd do anything she could to keep them out of harm's way, even if it meant shipping them off to play with penguins in Antarctica.

She was about to nod when the back door opened and Uncle Stan strode back into the kitchen. He looked upset and Mel knew he'd be thinking the exact same thing as everyone else. That she had to go underground.

"How are you doing, kid?" he asked.

"Not great," Mel said. "Everyone seems to think I need to go into hiding and I don't want to be difficult but it seems like overkill."

Joe winced and she said, "Sorry, unintended."

Uncle Stan nodded. "It might be for the best—just for a day or two."

"But—" Mel started to protest but Uncle Stan cut her off.

"I'm sure you don't want to put any of your people in harm's way by staying here, do you?"

He had her and he knew it.

"No," she said.

"All right," he said. "I'll call and make the arrangements."

"I'll take her home to pack a bag," Joe said.

Mel wanted to kick up a fuss, but she didn't. Instead, she hugged each of her guys and said, "Lock up when you leave. Be careful."

"It's going to be okay," Tate said. He kissed her forehead.

But as they exited the bakery with Salazar and Margolis escorting them, Mel felt as if nothing would ever be the same again. Who had shot at her? And why? And more importantly, had they mistaken Naomi for her? Mel didn't think she could ever forgive herself if they had.

Eight

"Safe house," Mel muttered. "More like prison."

She was sequestered in a condominium on the fifth floor of a newly built high-rise along the bank of the canal in Old Town Scottsdale. On the upside, she was still in her neighborhood, but on the downside, absolutely no one that she loved was allowed to visit her. Except Dwight, whom she did not love at the moment, not even a little.

"You want some cheese with that whine?" he asked.

"I am not whining," Mel protested. "I am complaining very loudly."

"Neither of which is going to help the current situation," he said.

He glanced around the swanky apartment. "This is not like any safe house I've ever seen."

"You've seen safe houses?" she asked.

"Sure." He shrugged. "You know, on TV. I feel like Tate must have had something to do with this."

"Maybe," Mel said. "It wouldn't be the first time he's meddled."

"I'd think you'd be taking advantage of the time off to catch up on your sleep, watch some television, or hit the spa. They have one on the first floor. It looks amazing."

"This isn't time off," Mel said. "It's me being forced into hiding because the poor woman who owned the shop next to mine—"

Her words faltered. She didn't know what had happened to Naomi. She'd called Uncle Stan for an update but hadn't heard back yet. Last night, she'd slept in her own bed with Joe beside her and undercover cops stationed outside their house. This morning, Joe had packed her off with a kiss on the lips, an "I love you," and a promise to check in with her throughout the day. So far, she'd heard from him only once and that was just to make sure she and Dwight hadn't murdered each other.

While Dwight tapped away on his laptop, she paced. She wanted to know what had happened to Naomi but no one was talking. Margolis and Salazar had dropped her off at the safe house and an undercover was on the premises, keeping watch.

She hadn't spoken to Uncle Stan and he wasn't answering her calls. She wondered if he knew she wanted to know about Naomi's condition and he was avoiding her. Well, it wasn't going to work. She picked up her cell phone and texted her uncle. In seconds, her phone rang. She put it on speakerphone since Dwight was staring at her with one eyebrow raised, clearly wanting to know whom she was calling and why.

"What do you mean you're going to tell on me?" Uncle Stan demanded.

"I'm going to tell Mom that you've got me at a safe house and you won't tell me what's happening," Mel said.

"You're bluffing," he said. "You'd never be so selfish as to make her worry like that."

"I might," she said.

"No, you wouldn't," Uncle Stan and Dwight said at the same time.

"Just tell me how Naomi is," Mel said. "Is she all right?"

There was a pause. It was the sort of silence that was so heavily loaded, it had actual weight to it. Mel gasped.

"She didn't make it," Mel said. She was stricken. She stared uncomprehendingly at Dwight and then handed him the phone, letting it slide out of her numb fingers and into his big mitt. "I need a minute."

She swallowed hard and made her way out to the terrace. She'd been told not to go out there but Mel didn't care. She was feeling claustrophobic and needed air. She could hear the rumble of Dwight's voice behind her as she closed the door.

She slumped onto one of the two padded lounge chairs in the shade of a small potted orange tree. It had finished blooming but the distinctive scent of its flowers perfumed the air around the tree. Normally, it was a scent that made Mel happy. Today, it made her sick.

Naomi Sutter was dead. If what everyone believed was true—that the shooter had been after Mel—then it was her fault that Naomi was dead. Mel put her head in her hands. How was she supposed to live with that?

Naomi had been so nice and charming and opening her soap shop had been her dream. Now it was all gone? Why? Who had done this?

Tears were falling before Mel even realized she was crying. She hadn't known Naomi well, but she'd liked her and the horrifying thought that her death might have something to do with Mel—that Mel might be responsible—made Naomi's loss simply unbearable.

"You all right?" Dwight asked.

Mel didn't look up. She couldn't. She was too wrecked.

"I'm fine," she said.

"You don't sound fine," he said. He pressed a cold bottle of water against the back of her hand.

Mel started. She took the water and the tissue he held in his other hand. He sat in the seat beside hers and studied her.

"Before you go making yourself all crazy," he said, "let's remember that we don't know that she was mistaken for you. That's just a theory. We know nothing about Naomi Sutter except the fact that she just opened a soap shop next door to your bakery. It could be a front for a money laundering scheme, or maybe she has a crazy ex-husband in the picture, or possibly her husband is cheating and either he decided this was his only way out or his side piece got tired of waiting for him to leave his wife and planned to expedite matters."

Mel dabbed her cheeks and blew her nose. She uncapped the water and took a long drink. When she lowered the bottle, she studied him and asked, "Exactly how much crime television do you watch anyway?"

"Enough to know that there is always more to the situation than what you see on the surface," he said. "You're just going to have to be patient while the police figure this out."

"But if I'm somehow responsible—" Mel began but Dwight interrupted her.

"Did you pull the trigger?" he asked.

"No."

"Then you're not responsible," he said. "Period. Case closed."

The tips of his ears were turning pink and Mel knew that meant that Dwight was feeling very strongly about what he was saying. She supposed she could have argued some more but it wasn't like it was an argument she wanted to win. She sincerely hoped he was right and maybe there was another reason Naomi had been murdered, which felt like an awful thing to think. She shivered.

"Come on," Dwight said. "Let's get back to work. The only way we're going to know for certain that the killer isn't someone from your past is to track them all down and see what they've been up to."

Mel nodded. He was right. If she had to be stuck in this safe house then the best thing she could do was make herself useful, tracking down leads. This was what no cop shows talked about. The sheer drudgery of tracking suspects. They were never where they were supposed to be and they were never happy to be found if they were trying to put some distance between their past criming and their present situation, particularly if they were still breaking the law.

"Are you sure you're up to this?" Mel asked. "I mean, you might be putting yourself in danger."

"'Danger is my middle name,'" Dwight said.

Mel laughed. "That's funny, Austin Powers."

Dwight stared at her. "No, seriously, Margie Danger married Dwight Pickard and they made my middle name Danger."

"Seriously?"

He nodded. He looked pained and Mel felt terrible for laughing.

"Well, okay, then," Mel said. "I guess Danger really is your middle name. Sorry I laughed."

Dwight nodded and then burst out laughing.

Mel frowned. "You were joking."

"And you believed me, you rube," he said. He snorted as if he couldn't believe that she had fallen for it.

"So what is your middle name?" she asked.

The humor vanished from his face. Wiped clean immediately. He rose from his seat and went back into the suite. In the doorway, he turned around and barked, "Come on, back to work."

Mel watched him disappear inside. She stood up and followed him. His middle name must be truly awful if he was refusing to answer her question. Well, now she had to know what it was.

"Vladimir," she said as she stepped inside.

Dwight ignored her. He sat down at the table in front of his laptop and pushed the legal pad they'd been using to list potential shooters toward her.

"Melvin," she guessed.

His jaw tightened and she wondered if she was getting warmer.

"Barnaby."

He let out a sigh and stared at her over the top of the computer. "I'm not telling you."

"Oh, it must be really bad," she said. "Give me a hint."

"No," he said. "If you're so smart, figure it out yourself."

"I will," she said.

She glanced down at the pad. Her tears had dried up and she was staring at the list while her brain churned through possibilities. It hit her then that he had done this on purpose to give her something else to think about and snap her out of her upset.

She glanced up at him. He was studying something on the screen.

"Thanks," she said.

"For what?" he asked.

"You know," she said.

He met her gaze and his eyes were kind. He nodded once and then went back to the computer. They spent the rest of the morning working through the list of suspects and every time Mel started to get weepy or upset, she offered another name that she suspected he would hate.

"Hieronymus," she said.

"Now you're just being mean."

He tapped the notepad. "Read back to me what we have so far."

She glanced down at the notebook. "We've verified the whereabouts of Christie Stevens's murderer and determined that there was no one who would seek vengeance on their behalf. The same for Baxter Malloy, Ty Stokes, Cassidy Havers, Vic Mazzotta, Sam Kelleher, and Mariel Mars. There are a few more to go."

"A few?" Dwight asked. "You really need to consider living on an island in the middle of the ocean all alone."

"Sounds fun," Mel retorted. "Byron?"

"Yeah, cause I'm a poet and you didn't know it."

Mel smiled. A knock at the door interrupted whatever retort she was about to make.

She and Dwight exchanged a look. This wasn't the knock that the undercover officer had told them he would use. His had been three short raps followed by three long ones. This was merely *bang, bang, bang* as if the person at the door was out of patience.

"Get down," Dwight ordered.

His face was immediately set and serious and Mel knew that this was Dwight the former soldier. She slipped out of her chair and down to the floor. He followed. They sat together staring at the door.

Mel could hear her blood pounding in her ears. Her breathing was rapid and a sheen of sweat coated her palms. How had the shooter found her?

"All right, here's what you're going to do," Dwight said. "I want you to crawl on all fours down the hallway to the farthest bedroom and call the number our officer friend had us put in our phones in case of an emergency. Can you do that?"

Mel sucked in a gulp of air and nodded. This wasn't a drill. There was someone outside. Someone who potentially wanted to shoot her and could harm Dwight in the process. She absolutely could not have another victim on her conscience.

"Okay, roll out!" Dwight ordered.

"But what about you?" she protested.

"I'm going to check the door," he said.

"Are you crazy? They could shoot you through the door."

"They're not going to shoot me through the door," he said. Judging by his annoyed expression, it was physically killing him not to roll his eyes.

"How do you know?" she persisted. She gestured to the wood. "They could totally shoot through that."

Dwight made a shooing motion with his hands. "Go."

Bang, bang, bang. The knock sounded again and Mel yelped.

"Shhh," Dwight hushed her. Again, he made a motion for her to shoo while he crept to the door. He was as stealthy as a cat and Mel admired the way a man as big as he was moved so silently.

"Hey, these meatballs are getting cold," a voice shouted through the door. "How long are you going to make me wait before you open up?"

Dwight looked confused and Mel sighed. She'd know that voice anywhere. And the subtle scent of garlic and oregano wafting through the door clinched it. She collapsed in relief against the floor. "It's Ray DeLaura."

"Angie's brother?"

"The one and only," she confirmed. "Thank goodness."

Dwight strode to the door and stared through the peephole. He shook his head and ran a hand over his buzz cut, then yanked the door open and demanded, "What are you doing here?"

"Ma made meatballs for Mel," Ray said. "She was worried Mel would be hungry."

He said it as if it was the most obvious thing in the world.

Dwight turned around and looked at Mel with an expression of *Do you believe this guy?*

Mel shrugged.

"How did you even find us?" Dwight asked. "This is supposed to be a secret safe house. Did anyone follow you?"

"Relax, I know what I'm doing. No one followed me," Ray said. He hefted an aluminum serving dish. "So are you letting me in or what?"

"Yes," Mel said at the same time Dwight said, "No."

Mel looked at Dwight. "Clearly you haven't had Mrs. DeLaura's meatballs if you just said no."

"Are they worth getting shot for?" Dwight asked.

"Yes," Mel and Ray said together.

Dwight stepped aside and let Ray into the suite.

Mel moved into the kitchenette and gathered plates and utensils.

"What brings you by, Ray?" Mel asked.

"Can't a guy check on his sis-in-law?"

"Of course you can," she said. "But no one is supposed to know where I am. If you wanted an update, you probably should have asked your girlfriend, Detective Martinez."

"She wasn't talking," he said.

"Or your brother," Dwight suggested.

"He wasn't talking, either," he said. "And he definitely wasn't taking my advice."

"Advice?" Mel asked. Yes, even though deep down she knew better, she went there anyway.

"Yeah." Ray put the meatballs on the counter and spread his hands wide. "I mean, here he is newly married and he lets his wife go into lockdown with another dude. Who does that?"

Mel felt her jaw drop open. She stared at him as if he'd just started speaking in tongues.

"Are you crazy?" she asked.

"As a bedbug," Dwight said.

"I am not a pest," Ray argued.

"Notice he didn't deny the crazy part," Dwight said.

"That, either," Ray said.

"Honestly, Ray, the thought that anything could happen between me and Dwight." Mel shook her head. She couldn't even look at Dwight for fear she'd dissolve into a puddle of embarrassment.

"Hey, you can never be too sure. What was that movie with the guy from the baseball movie protecting the singer?"

"*The Bodyguard*?" Dwight asked.

"Yeah," Ray said. "A dangerous circumstance can make people feel things they shouldn't, that's all I'm saying."

Mel closed her eyes and prayed for patience. "Trust me, this is not a concern."

"Yeah," Dwight agreed. "She's no Whitney Houston."

Mel frowned and shot back, "Well, you're no Kevin Costner."

"Whatever," he said.

Ray glanced between them and said, "See? This is exactly how it starts."

"Shut up," they both snapped.

"Don't shoot the messenger," he said. "Especially when he brought meatballs."

He peeled off the lid and Mel was immediately remorseful. The DeLaura meatballs would do that for a gal.

"I'm sorry," she said. "But you really didn't have to worry. Dwight and I are friends, good friends."

Ray looked skeptical.

"Yeah," Dwight agreed. "A friendship forged on getting shot at together. You can't beat that."

"Unless you're family who's been shot at together," Ray said. He sounded a teeny bit superior.

Dwight scoffed. "For real, Cooper? You've been shot at with him, too?"

Mel shrugged. There really wasn't anything she could say here. She decided to change the subject.

"Do they know who shot Naomi?" Her voice was high and tight.

"No, but the entire Old Town community thinks that she was mistaken for you and that's why she got shot," he said.

Mel sat down hard in her chair. Dwight frowned at Ray. "Now you've done it, she's going to want to break out of here."

"Why?" Ray countered. "These are pretty sweet digs."

Bang, bang, bang. Another knock sounded on the door.

"I'll get it," Ray said.

"Wait," Dwight said. "It could be the shooter."

"Nah, I think it's Paulie with the bread," Ray said.

"Bread?"

"You can't have meatballs without garlic bread," Ray answered. "It's simply unnatural."

Mel glanced at Dwight. "I don't think our secret safe house is so secret anymore."

"Or safe." He ran a hand over his eyes.

Nine

Standing outside with Paulie, who was indeed carrying bread, was the undercover officer charged with keeping them safe. He frowned at Paulie and Ray and then came inside the suite. "I'm calling Stan."

"Now you've done it," Mel said to the brothers.

Personally, she was thrilled. She didn't want to spend the next few days in a safe house not knowing what was happening. She began to scoop out meatballs and her gaze met Ray's. He gave her a slow wink and she realized he had barged into her safe house on purpose. She knew he would never put her in harm's way, so there had to be a reason that he was disrupting her stay at the safe house. Oh, good grief, he wasn't actually worried about her and Dwight, was he?

The undercover officer was cajoled into eating, while keeping his eye on the door. Mel maneuvered Ray into the corner of the kitchen and asked, "What gives? You know Joe is going to be furious."

Ray shrugged. "Probably, but I don't think this safe house is that safe, not if I can figure out where it is."

"How did you figure it out?"

"I know a guy," he said.

Ray always "knew a guy."

"And?" Mel badgered.

Ray shrugged. "He owns the building. He was a little freaked out that the police wanted one of the condos to house a person tied to a murder so he reached out to me to see what I know," Ray said. "When he described the situation, I figured it was you."

"What did you tell him?" Mel asked.

"I said I'd look into it, but if he's asking me, he's asking others, which means this place is not safe and you need to get out of here," he said. He eyed the undercover cop suspiciously.

"Stop. He's fine," Mel said. "Uncle Stan chose him specifically."

Ray's scowl at the officer lessened exactly one degree and then returned to Mel.

"Tara's going to murder you," she said, and she didn't think it was hyperbole.

"Keeps things exciting," Ray said. He waggled his eyebrows and Mel sighed. "Besides, if I hadn't figured it out, Tony would have."

"Assuming he hasn't already," Mel agreed. Tony was the brother who was a technological wiz but also lived a life that no one quite understood. His occupational title was vague, his relationship status murky, and his ability to track the rest of the family uncanny. Mel wondered if he'd had them all microchipped, like pets, when they were sleeping.

"So, what's the plan?" she asked.

"You mean after Stan comes and yells at all of us?"

"Yeah."

"I think we—and by 'we' I mean you—need to attend the gathering that the Old Town Small Business Association is having for Naomi tonight. Apparently, John Billings felt that it was important that everyone pull together as a community. They're organizing a fund-raiser to help her husband with the medical and funeral expenses."

Mel felt all of the blood rush from her head and she was rocked with a bout of dizziness. This was real. Naomi was gone. Fund-raisers were happening in her name. It was simply a nightmare.

"Why do you think I should be there?" Mel asked. She had to swallow the lump in her throat to continue. "I mean, given that half of the local businesses want to shut us down, I'm not sure it's appropriate for me to attend. Plus, her husband must be devastated. I don't think I can face him if she was shot because she was mistaken for me."

Ray crossed his arms over his chest. "I didn't think you were a coward."

"Well, now you know otherwise," she said. "Listen, I don't want to upset anyone and I don't think my being there is going to help the situation."

"Of course it will. Besides, I don't think her husband is going to be there," he said. "I imagine he's dealing with a lot right now."

"I don't know," Mel said. She didn't think she could handle Nikki Guthrie and her petition-signing posse at the moment.

"You have to. Listen, if I've learned one thing from all of my murder mystery reading, it's that the killer is always at the victim's wake or funeral or fund-raiser," he said.

"You read murder mysteries?" Mel asked. How had she not known this?

"Every night before bed," he said. "It helps me sleep, especially the traditional mysteries where you know good will triumph over evil."

"Huh." Mel had no idea what to do with this information. "I get the theory," she said. "But if the shooter killed Naomi by mistake would they still show up?"

"Yes," Ray said. "Especially if you're there and you were the intended victim."

"Joe is never going to go for this," she said.

"I don't see why not," Ray said. "All the brothers will be there and we can protect you better than anyone else."

"How do you figure?"

"You're fam and we protect our own," he said, as if this was obvious.

Mel's heart went smoosh. She had to admit that marrying Joe had given her more family than she'd ever bargained on and she couldn't be happier about it.

Bang bang bang.

"Looks like we're about to find out if your plan is a go," Mel said.

Uncle Stan was less than thrilled with Ray. In fact, he was furious. He and Joe arrived within minutes of each other and while consuming a healthy portion of meatballs, Stan ranted and raved and read Ray the riot act while Joe nodded. For Ray's part, he enjoyed another helping of meatballs.

"What were you thinking?" Uncle Stan shouted.

"I was thinking Mel needs to be at the gathering for Naomi tonight, not locked away here doing nothing, where anyone can find her and shoot her," Ray said. "You can put her in a Kevlar vest and we'll make sure she is surrounded by DeLauras at all times."

"No," Mel said. "Absolutely not. I couldn't bear it if anyone was harmed while protecting me. Besides, I really don't think the shooter is going to do anything at the fund-raiser. I mean it's not like it's the wake or the funeral."

"Be that as it may, we won't know unless you go," Ray said.

They were all silent, mulling over the situation. Judging by the looks on all of their faces, Mel could tell none of them was pleased.

"I know I can't tell you what to do, but I don't want you to do this," Joe said.

Mel put her hand on his shoulder, knowing she'd feel the exact same way if the situation was reversed.

"Hiding isn't going to make the shooter go away," she said. She glanced at her uncle, who was surprisingly silent. "I think I need to try to draw them out, for Naomi."

"You're right." Uncle Stan nodded. "We haven't been able to track down the car Oz saw even with the partial plate. There are just too many license plates that end in N8. We need to do something." He glanced at her from beneath a furrowed brow. He was clearly feeling conflicted. "Your mother is going to kill me."

"More meatballs?" Ray asked. He held up the ladle

and Stan waved it in with the desperation of a man consuming his last meal.

\\'/\'/\\

Mel sat in the middle of a row of hastily set-up
folding chairs, surrounded by DeLauras. Angie had been
ordered to stay home, which she'd fussed about until Tate
said that Emari needed her mama. Full stop. Then Angie
settled, accepting that her new role as a mother was her
number one priority. She made Tate promise to call her
and let her listen to the event on speakerphone so that she
knew what was going on.

Naomi's soap shop, where the gathering was being
held, was packed. Naomi's husband, David, wasn't in attendance but her assistant, Pam, was. Judging by her red-
rimmed eyes, she was struggling to process the events of
the night before. Mel wanted to go hug her but held back,
not knowing how she'd be received. If Pam took a swing
at her, she wouldn't blame the woman.

Mel wasn't surprised by David's absence. The poor
man's life had just been destroyed. She wondered how he
was doing and if there was anything she could do to help.
Somehow, a delivery of cupcakes seemed entirely too
cheerful, given the circumstance. Perhaps she'd blow the
dust off her old cookbooks and bake him something more
substantial, like a cheese soufflé or a carrot cake.

Ray, who'd been gathering information, told Mel that
Naomi and David had married late and never had children. Mel had met David only once. He was tall and thin
and, if she remembered right, worked in retail at a men's
suit store. It made sense because the day they'd met he'd

been wearing a charcoal gray suit that was obviously bespoke, as it fit his lean frame to perfection.

His gray hair was side parted and combed over the thin spots on top of his head. His glasses were large and he pushed them up his nose in a gesture that seemed more habit than necessity. He and Naomi had seemed an unlikely couple, but Naomi always smiled when she mentioned her husband's name so Mel had gotten the feeling that they were very fond of each other. Not just spouses but also friends. Mel's heart broke for him.

John's speech was short but his deep voice and mustache sold it and there were a few heartfelt sobs in the crowd. Mel glanced around and noticed that most of the Old Town businesspeople were in attendance, which was surprising only because Naomi had been relatively new. Then again, she'd been shot so there was a certain macabre interest in the circumstances surrounding her murder.

Mel lowered her head as that fact hit her square in the face again. Naomi with her twinkling eyes and quick wit was gone. Mel had felt a kinship with her and the regret at the loss of a future friendship was acute.

"On behalf of the Sutter family, we'll be taking donations in memory of Naomi," John said. "It's a tragic thing to lose a loved one so senselessly and so young. I'm sure David will appreciate any support you can give him."

The music piped in over the shop's loudspeaker was a gentle jazz melody. Mel wondered what Naomi would have thought of it. The guests rose to their feet and began to mingle. Mel didn't think she was imagining the whispers that followed her as she made her way to John.

It was difficult to navigate the crowd while surrounded

by a circle of DeLauras. Joe was by her side while Ray, Paulie, Tony, and Al each took point. It was like trying to move in a potato sack race, all of the moving parts had to move together. As it was, she slammed into Ray's back, Tony crashed into her, and they all teetered on the brink of falling when Joe grabbed her about the waist and steadied her.

Mel saw Uncle Stan watching from one side of the room, looking equal parts embarrassed for her and embarrassed to know her. Mel couldn't fault him. Meanwhile, Tara, his partner and Ray's girlfriend, stood on the other side of the room and pretended not to know any of them. Mel didn't blame her a bit.

Several plainclothes officers were mixed in among the attendees, and truly Mel couldn't have felt safer or more suffocated, since they'd also put her in a five-pound Kevlar vest that was like wearing a weighted blanket around her middle.

She had almost reached John when a man stepped into their path. Jacob Wright, who owned an import business, stopped their progress. He was short, stout, and very red in the face. He was also not at all intimidated by the brothers as he glared past them right at Mel.

"You have some nerve showing up here," he said.

"Excuse me?" Mel asked. Her voice was shaky and Joe put a hand on her lower back to steady her. Jacob Wright had always greeted Mel with a smile and a wave before today. She frequently shopped at his import store and he always ordered specialty cupcakes for his wife Kayleigh's birthdays.

"You heard me," Jacob snapped. "Naomi Sutter is dead because of you."

"Hey, settle down," Joe said. His voice wasn't shaky at all but rather sounded like a growl of fury.

"No, I won't settle," Jacob said. "Nikki Guthrie is right. You're a menace to our community and you need to be gone."

Mel glanced past him and saw Nikki, looking quite pleased with herself. She turned back to Jacob, feeling deeply hurt, and said, "I'm sorry you feel that way—"

"Don't apologize to me," he said. "Apologize to Naomi, since you're the reason she's dead."

"Stop saying that," Mel said. "I didn't shoot her. I had nothing to do with her death."

"So, someone just happened to shoot at you and then the next night, a woman who owns the shop next door to you, who looks like you, is shot and killed?" Jacob asked. He waved his hands in the air. "Total coincidence."

Mel knew it sounded bad and when she glanced at the other business owners in the shop, she noticed none of them would meet her gaze. It looked like Nikki was going to get her way. Even the shop owners who'd believed in her before seemed to be rethinking their opinion since Naomi had been murdered. Everyone except Mick. He stood at the front of the room with John and when he met Mel's gaze, he nodded at her, letting her know he was still on her side.

"Listen, I don't know what happened," Mel said. "I don't know why Naomi was shot or why I was shot at. The only thing I do know is that there's a killer out there, and I, for one, won't rest until they are brought to justice."

"Hell, yeah!" Ray cheered.

Mel's speech did not have the rousing effect she had hoped for. Instead, the mutters and murmurs of the crowd seemed to get louder and uglier.

John Billings broke away from the other board members and approached Mel's group. His face was kindly but also sad. Even his mustache drooped.

"I'm sorry, Mel, I know you mean well, but maybe it's best if you go," he said.

"But I want to contribute," Mel said. "I want to help Naomi's husband."

"Haven't you done enough?" Nikki Guthrie asked. She was wearing a dark blue suit and spiked heels. "Incidentally, I have enough signatures on my petition. Your bakery is history."

"Why are you so intent on ruining my business?" Mel asked before any of the brothers could speak. "Haven't I always been a contributing member of the association? Tate, Angie, and I built our bakery up from scratch—"

"Ha! That's rich," Jacob cackled. "And I do mean *rich*."

"What the hell is that supposed to mean?" Tate asked, bringing up the rear of their group.

"What do you think it means, rich boy?" Jacob asked. He stretched himself up, trying to look Tate in the eye, but he was still six inches shorter than the shortest DeLaura, who was Ray. "You've never had to struggle. You've always had money. You opened that bakery bankrolled by your rich daddy and you've never known what it was like to try and survive when times got tough."

"I earned every penny that I invested in our bakery," Tate said. "And, yes, I come from an investment background, but I didn't have anything handed to me. I worked for every bit of it."

"Sure you did," Jacob said. His tone was snide and he rolled his eyes at Nikki, who smirked.

"Hey, man, it's not my fault if you don't know how to

turn a profit in a tourist-loaded area like Scottsdale," Tate said. "Here's a thought, maybe you need to go work for someone who knows what they're doing—"

Mel stepped on his foot.

"Ouch!" Tate said.

"Sorry," Mel said. She wasn't. Nothing that was coming out of Tate's mouth was going to help them right now and she didn't want him to do any damage that couldn't be undone.

"Time to go," Joe said.

"Yup," Tony said. He began to shuffle-walk their group to the door.

"Can you believe the nerve of that guy?" Tate asked Mel.

"I feel like he's not alone," she said. She glanced around the shop at the people she'd known for years who she'd thought were their friends. "In fact, I'm surprised they're not chasing us out of here with torches and pitchforks."

"I had no idea that the other business owners felt this way about the bakery, did you?" Tate asked. He sounded hurt and Mel knew exactly how he felt.

"No," she said. She curled her hand around his elbow and matched her stride to his as they left the soap shop within the protective circle of their in-laws.

> \' \ \ '

"I want to see David," Mel said. "I just need to talk to him and tell him how sorry I am."

She was standing in the kitchen of the bakery while the rest of the entourage was out front, helping Marty, whether he liked it or not.

Uncle Stan looked pained. "I'm sorry, kid. You're going to have to wait. There's an ongoing investigation and as Naomi's spouse, he's a part of it, plus, I doubt he'll want to talk to anyone right now."

"I just need to know . . ." Mel's voice trailed off. She couldn't get the words out.

"If he blames you for his wife being shot?" Uncle Stan asked.

"Yeah," she said.

"From the time I've spent interviewing him, I'd say that's a no," Uncle Stan said. "He seems to think it was a random act of violence and that Naomi was in the wrong place at the wrong time just like you."

Mel stared at the top of the steel worktable. She wanted that to be true so badly she could taste it.

"Hey, kid."

Mel glanced up.

Uncle Stan's eyes were soft with compassion. "No matter what we find out. This isn't your fault. The responsibility belongs solely to the shooter."

Intellectually Mel knew this, but still, a shooting from a mistaken identity, from a bad guy believing that Naomi was her, well, it was going to be tough to take if it was true.

"Go home and get some sleep," Uncle Stan said.

Mel glanced at him. "You're letting me go home? To my house?"

He smiled. "Yeah. If Ray can find you, then the only way to keep you safe would be to send you out of state and I'm guessing you'd refuse."

"Correct."

"That's what I figured," he said. "You might as well go home, where at least I'll know where you are."

"You have the entire neighborhood under surveillance, don't you?"

"If a stray cat so much as jumps into your yard, we'll know," he said.

"Did my mom put you up to that?" Mel asked.

"She didn't have to," he said. "No one is going to get to you. Not under my watch."

Mel circled the table and hugged him hard. Uncle Stan hugged her back and then cleared his throat. "Come on, you'd better collect those DeLaura brothers before they eat all of the cupcakes in your display."

Mel nodded. While the others had consoled themselves with cupcakes, she'd stayed in the kitchen with Uncle Stan. For the first time in her life, she was suffering in a way not even a cupcake could cure. Naomi couldn't have died because of Mel. She just couldn't. And Mel was going to do everything she could to prove that she didn't.

Ten

Mel brooded all night about Naomi and the pushback she was getting from the other business owners in the district. She did not sleep well and woke up with a case of bedhead that looked like she'd gone through a car wash with the windows down. It wasn't a great start to the day.

Over coffee, lots of coffee, she told Joe she was going to visit the business owners she considered friends in Old Town and try to get some answers. To her surprise, Joe glanced at her over the rim of his mug and said, "Where do we start?"

"We? You're coming with me?"

"Cupcake, just because you were released from the safe house doesn't mean you're not in danger," he said.

"Until we know that Naomi's shooting had nothing to do with you, I'm not letting you out of my sight."

"I have a feeling you're only going along with this because you know Uncle Stan has me under surveillance."

"Yup."

"Is he going to be okay with me leaving the house?" she asked.

"He expected nothing less," Joe said. "And neither did I."

"Now it's all coming into focus," Mel said. "You and Uncle Stan knew I was going to go to Old Town today."

"We knew you wouldn't be able to not try and find out who shot Naomi," he corrected her. "So I promised Uncle Stan I'd be with you at all times."

Mel realized she was a lucky person to have such stand-up men in her life. "I love you."

He smiled. "I love you, too."

\'\.'\ '\

"Hey, Mick," Mel greeted the tattoo parlor owner as she entered his shop. "Are you busy?"

Mick was lounging on the couch in the corner. The television was on and he was watching a soccer match. He turned his head when she stepped inside with Joe right behind her. The brothers, Ray and Al, were left to wait outside. Mel noticed that they each stood on one side of the door, with their legs spread wide and their hands clasped in front of them as if they were a security team on a detail. Thankfully, Dwight had stayed behind at the bakery to keep doing research online. There were several family members of murderers Mel had helped catch that were unaccounted for and he was doing his best to locate them.

"I always have time for you," Mick said. He stood up and gestured for them to take the couch beside his. "What's up?"

"First, as a thank-you for not turning against me and the bakery and for refusing to sign the petition to get us booted, I brought you some vegan coconut cupcakes," she said. Mick had recently gone full vegan and Mel knew her coconut cupcakes were his favorite.

She held out the box to him and his eyes lit up. He popped the lid and peered inside.

"Aw, thanks, these look amazing. But you didn't have to do that. I'll always have your back. What's happening in our community is wrong. We're supposed to support each other. I really thought we were better than this."

"You aren't alone there," Joe said. They exchanged a look of understanding.

Mick lifted a cupcake out of the four-pack, which looked ridiculously small in his large tattooed hands. "Is it okay if I have one now? I just finished with a client. I'm doing eagle wings on his back. It's beautiful but exhausting and I'm starving."

"Go for it," Mel said. She felt the same thrill she always did when her baked goods made someone happy. Being able to give comfort, joy, or sustenance was an excellent way to make a living.

"Oh my god, so good," Mick said through a mouthful. He polished off the entire cupcake in three bites. "How do you make the frosting and still keep it vegan without butter or milk?"

"It's a combination of coconut oil and vegan butter," Mel said. She grinned. "I have mad skills."

"I'll say," Mick said. He eyed the box as if he was thinking about having another but shook his head and focused on them. "Not to bring up a sad subject, but have you heard anything about the shooter?"

"Not yet," Mel said. "Listen, I don't want to put you on the spot, and I don't mean to brood, but I was really surprised by the hostility of some of our neighbors. I mean, Nikki with her petition and Jacob was so angry. I have to know, how long have they felt this way?"

Mick shrugged. "It's the first I've ever heard of it but then everyone knows we're friends so maybe they wouldn't share that with me."

Mel nodded. That made sense but it didn't help her information gathering.

"How far do you think Naomi and Jacob would go to drive us out?" Mel asked.

"Are you asking if I think they'd shoot you to get rid of you?"

"I guess I am." Mel hated to admit it, but it was one of the concerns that had kept her up all night.

"I don't know. That's a pretty big leap to make from being bitter about your success. There is one thing." Mick paused. "I don't want to talk out of turn, but I heard some conversations that lead me to believe that some of our struggling neighborhood businesses might be taking out high-interest loans that they can't afford to pay back, in order to stay afloat."

"Nikki? Jacob?" Mel asked.

Mick nodded. "Among others."

"That would certainly explain their resentment," Joe said. "Money, or the lack of it, makes people stressed and mean."

"Agreed," Mick said. "Worrying about how you're going to keep the lights on and eat can really take the joy out of self-employment."

"You sound as if you've walked the walk," Mel said.

Mick nodded. "It was two years before I turned a profit in this shop, and I'm not talking a big profit. Just one large enough to justify staying open for another year and then another year. Luckily, the business eventually took off."

"And now look at you," Mel said. "You were chosen as the Scottsdale Business Person of the Year."

A faint pink blush stained his cheeks and Mick looked a bit embarrassed. The award couldn't have been given to a nicer guy. Mick was like the babysitter of the neighborhood. No one else cared as much as he did about Old Town.

"It should have been you," he said. "Your trajectory has been amazing and I believe it would have been with or without Tate's initial investment. Your cupcakes are legendary."

"Thanks, Mick," Mel said. "I like to think that's true, but honestly I did have a head start and the security to take chances in the beginning that a lot of start-ups don't have."

"You know who you might want to talk to is Mindy Rios, the owner of the Triple Fork Saloon, she hears everything," Mick said.

Mel nodded. She and Mick had been to the Triple Fork together a while back when Mel was tied up in another investigation. It was a western-style bar in the heart of Old Town and while she didn't usually day-drink, today she might make an exception.

"Good idea," she said. "If you hear anything else that might be of interest, let us know."

"Count on it," he said.

They left the tattoo parlor and Mel looked at Joe. "Too early for a whiskey?"

"What?" Ray asked as he and Al pushed away from their spots on either side of the door. "It's never too early for a whiskey."

Joe gave him a look and Ray shrugged. No remorse.

They stopped by the bakery and Mel chose a four-pack of chocolate cupcakes with vanilla icing. It was the bakery's most popular flavor and she knew a straight shooter like Mindy Rios would definitely go for them. No, she was not above bribery with baked goods.

They crossed the street and walked along the opposite sidewalk until they reached the Triple Fork Saloon. A popular tourist spot, with live music every night, the saloon definitely had a Wild West feel to it and it wasn't just the glass-topped tables made from wagon wheels.

Aside from a couple playing darts and some tourists sitting on the barstools shaped like saddles, the joint was empty. Mel approached the bar and greeted Travis the bartender.

"Hey, Trav," she said. "Is Mindy around?"

"In the office," he said. "You can go ahead. She's doing payroll and talking to beer distributors, both of which she hates. She'll be happy for the interruption."

"Thanks," Mel said. She turned to Joe. "Why don't you guys wait here? Mindy might talk more easily just to me."

"This is where being a prosecutor might be an asset," Joe said.

"We're not here for an interrogation. Besides, she's never had trouble with the law," Mel said. "At least, not that I know of, but officers of the court and bar owners don't have a lot of common ground."

"Understood," he said. "I'm going to get a Coke, you want one?"

"Yes, please," Mel said. So, no day-drinking, then.

She stepped into the narrow dark hallway in the corner of the saloon that led to Mindy's office. She knocked and waited until she heard "Come in" before she opened the door.

Mindy Rios was seated behind the desk with the phone to her ear. She gestured that she just needed a minute on the phone and waved Mel in.

"It's a huge event night with five local bands on an outside stage," Mindy said. "I'm going to need more kegs than that."

Mindy's office was light and bright and signed framed photographs of all of the local bands who'd played the saloon were on the walls. Mel paused to admire the pictures while she waited. There were the Cartwheels—cute lead singer!—the Rita Rose Trio, Dimestore Western, and Honeygirl. Mel had seen several of these bands since she, Angie, and Tate used to come to the saloon for a drink or two after a long day of setting up the bakery. Life had become a bit too busy for that kind of spontaneous end-of-the-day wind-down and she felt a pang of nostalgia for the good old days. This was one of those moments when it occurred to her that adulthood was way overrated.

"Mel, sorry about that. How are you?" Mindy asked as she ended her call and tossed her cell phone onto the desk.

Mel pointed with her thumb at the wall. "Right now I'm missing my youth."

Mindy laughed. "Yup, you and the gang used to be regulars. Tate always wore that terrible cowboy hat."

"And Angie wore the highest boots she could find," Mel laughed. She sat in the chair opposite Mindy's and pushed the cupcakes across the desk toward her. "We were ridiculous."

"Nah, you're still some of my favorite customers," Mindy said. She glanced at the box and rubbed her hands together. "And not just because you bring goodies when you come by."

She had long silver hair that she wore in a fat braid that hung halfway down her back. Despite the gray, her face was unlined and she wore chunky turquoise-and-silver jewelry at her wrists and throat, which went well with her sleeveless plaid western shirt and jeans.

"Well, the Triple Fork was our watering hole for many years," Mel said. "Then we all grew up and became responsible adults."

"Yuck." Mindy shook her head. "One star. I do not recommend."

Mel laughed. "Agreed, and given the week I've had, don't be surprised if you see me perched on a stool on Friday night."

"Everyone comes home eventually," Mindy said. Her face grew shadowed and she said, "Unless you're Naomi Sutter, I guess."

Mel nodded. "I still can't believe that happened."

"Is your uncle working the case?"

Mel nodded. "No leads as far as I know."

"I heard you got shot at, too," Mindy said. Her soft brown eyes were worried. "That had to be terrifying. I'm so sorry. I saw you at the fund-raiser last night. Jacob Wright is a horse's ass. Don't let whatever nonsense he was saying bother you."

"I'm trying not to," Mel said. "I was just talking to Mick about it, in fact. He said that there's some bad feelings toward the bakery because we're doing well financially."

"Not your fault cupcakes sell," Mindy said. She shrugged. "They're a lot like beer. We can't help it if we chose our businesses wisely."

"Mick seemed to think some of the businesses were getting in over their heads in bad loans." Mel watched as Mindy pursed her lips and nodded.

"I might have heard something like that," she said. "There have been a few tales of woe in the bar recently. Jacob Wright in particular has been spending a lot of time in here."

"He does seem particularly angry."

"I heard him talking to a few of the other shop owners about a company called Business Equity Life," Mindy said. "It sounded sketchy to me, but he seemed to think it was the answer to his problems and he was encouraging the others to talk to the owner. What was his name?" She tapped her forefinger to her lip as she tried to remember. "Dale, no, Daniel, no . . . Dylan." She snapped her fingers. "Dylan Lewis, that was the name Jacob said."

"Interesting," Mel said. She made a mental note of the name. "I hope it works out for them because I could really use a de-escalation in the resentment they've been sending my way."

"I'd still watch my back if I were you," Mindy said. "For whatever reason, Nikki sure has it in for you with that ridiculous petition. I mean, seriously, drive away the successful local businesses, because, yeah, that makes sense."

"Right?" Mel said. "It truly boggles."

"Be careful out there, Mel," Mindy warned her. "I don't think you've heard the last from Jacob or Nikki. If she doesn't get her way with shutting you down, it wouldn't surprise me at all if she tries to ruin you by driving your customers away."

Mel frowned. "She can try."

"And she will," Mindy added. "I'll keep listening. If I pick up anything of interest, I'll be sure to let you know."

"I'd appreciate it."

Mel left the office with a wave and a promise to come see a live show soon.

Al and Ray were at the pool table and Joe was watching them from the bar. Mel sidled up to him and said, "We can go."

"Did you learn anything?" he asked. He handed her a glass of Coke, which she downed in a couple of swallows.

"Maybe," Mel said. "I'll tell you about it, but right now I need to get back to the bakery."

Hearing the urgency in her tone, Joe signaled to the bartender that he needed his tab. He paid and they headed out, barely giving Ray and Al time to catch up.

"What's going on, cupcake?" Joe asked. "You look worried."

"I am," she said. "Mindy warned me that Nikki is out to get the bakery. I hadn't realized how much animosity she had for us until this week. If the petition doesn't go through I'm afraid she'll try to hurt the business in other ways."

"What could she possibly do?" Ray asked.

"Bad online reviews, rumors, convincing customers not to order from us," Mel said. "There are endless ways to crush a business these days."

"But why?" Al said.

"Spite, fear, jealousy," Mel said. "Who knows? The bakery has been involved with enough local murder cases that she could have convinced herself that we really are a blight on the neighborhood."

"Which is crazy," Ray said.

"Is it? I'm not so sure anymore."

When they arrived at the bakery, it was deserted. At first Mel thought nothing of it. There was usually a daily lull, which the staff used to load up on caffeine to power through until closing. This was too early for the daily lull, however.

"Yes, ma'am," Oz said. He was on the bakery's phone. "I understand."

Mel glanced at him. He was standing behind the counter with Marty and their newest hire, Madison Jacobson. She was biting her fingernails as she leaned in to listen to the conversation, while Marty had his arms crossed over his chest, looking irked.

"Hi, what's—" Mel said but Marty held up a hand in a wait gesture. She glanced at Joe, who raised his eyebrows in question.

"That's an awfully big order to cancel at the last minute," Oz said. "We're unable to return your deposit as it's less than twenty-four hours until your event." There was a high-pitched, harsh-sounding voice coming from the phone, which Oz pulled away from his ear. "I'm sorry but the terms of canceling your order were spelled out in our agreement. I do hope you'll be able to find another bakery to accommodate you at the last minute." There was a pause and then he nodded and said, "You're going with pies. Interesting choice. Thank you for letting us know."

"Pies?" Madison curled her lip. "Who chooses pie over cupcakes?"

"What's going on?" Mel asked.

"We're being excommunicated," Marty said. "As in *See ya, good-bye, don't let the door hit you on the way out.*"

"What are you talking about?" Ray asked. "Excommunicated from what?"

"The community," Marty said. He elbowed Oz in the side. "Tell them."

"Ouch," Oz grunted. He rubbed his ribs and frowned

at Marty. "Those bony elbows of yours could be registered as lethal weapons. And quit panicking. It's just a few cancellations."

"A few?" Marty scoffed.

Mel felt her stomach twist into a knot. She was beginning to get nervous and sweaty. "You guys are freaking me out. Start from the beginning. Why do you think we're being excommunicated?"

"We're not," Oz insisted. "Shunned, perhaps."

"Shunned?!" Mel's voice came out in a squeak.

"Explain," Joe said.

"We've had a few cancellations today for special orders," Oz said. "The Reinhold retirement party, the Baskin-Kingsley wedding, the Kruger graduation, the Perkins baby shower, and the . . ."

He frowned, trying to remember.

"The Cordoba anniversary party," Madison said. She looked crushed. "There goes all of my Instagram material for the month."

Being a savvy teen, Madison had taken over the social media accounts while Angie was on maternity leave. For the first time in Mel's memory, the bubbly blond teen looked genuinely deflated.

"And this place is empty, like dead empty," Al said. Everyone turned to look at him. He looked immediately contrite. "Sorry, I'll just go eat a cupcake or something."

"I'll join you," Ray said. "Because clearly you're going to need someone to consume the stock."

Together, the brothers went into the kitchen.

Mel turned back to Oz and Marty. "Has it been like this all morning?"

Marty nodded.

"And we've had five cancellations?"

"Plus two orders yesterday that I didn't think were a big deal until now," Oz said. "Totaling seven."

"Seven?" Mel cried.

Madison's shoulders drooped and she heaved a heavy sigh. "It's true. We've been canceled."

Eleven

"Canceled?" Mel clutched the front of her shirt in anxiety.

"Easy, cupcake," Joe said. "This could be a coincidence."

"It's not," she said. "I feel it in my bones and I bet Nikki is at the root of all of this."

"Even if she is, does a marginal jewelry designer really have that much sway in the local community?"

"Are you kidding?" Marty asked. "She doesn't have to do anything but weaponize some social media posts. With the speed and tenacity of the Internet trolls these days, a business is only as successful as its last post."

"Oh, no, this is all my fault!" Madison wailed, and then turned and ran into the kitchen.

"Real smooth, there, Marty," Oz said. He spun on his heel and followed Madison.

"What did I say?" Marty asked. He turned back to Mel and Joe, looking for an explanation but Mel wasn't up for teaching an eightysomething-year-old man tact at the moment.

She crossed the bakery and sank into a booth, lying down on the bench and letting her feet hang out. She put her arm over her eyes and tried not to panic. Everything they'd worked for all of these years and now it was *poof!* Gone. What was she going to say to Tate and Angie? They had a family to provide for now. And what about all of their franchises? Would this shunning include them in their communities, too? Mel felt dizzy. The number of lives ruined and all because of Mel.

"Listen, I know you're worried and probably beating yourself up as if you had anything to do with this, but you didn't." Joe knelt in the booth beside hers and perched over the seat top to look down at her. "And it's going to be okay."

"How?" Mel asked. "How can it possibly ever be okay? We've been canceled—*canceled!*" Even to her own ears she sounded the teeniest bit hysterical.

"No, you're having a quiet day at the bakery, which is not a surprise given that there was a murder next door. Also, that could be why there were several cancellations. People tend to get cautious about going to places where there are shootings."

Mel lifted her arm off her face and stared up at him. There was her voice-of-reason husband, the mediator to his large brood of siblings, and all-around calming influence on the forces of chaos in his life.

"Thank you," she said. "I'm sure you must be right. It's just the natural fallout given the violence in the area. It's not us. I'll bet other businesses are suffering just as much."

She could practically hear Marty rolling his eyes from ten feet away.

"Exactly," Joe said.

"I still need to tell Tate and Angie what's happening," she said.

"Of course," her husband agreed. "Why don't you meet up with Angie at my parents' house? Uncle Stan has it under watch and there are so many DeLauras coming and going that even a bad guy would be too confused to attempt anything."

Mel appreciated his attempt at humor but she was hesitant to put any of her in-laws in danger. As if reading her mind, Joe grabbed her hand and gave it a reassuring squeeze. "It'll be okay, I promise."

\' \' , \' \'

"Stop swiveling your head around like that, you're going to strain something," Angie said.

"Sorry, I'm just trying to be aware of my surroundings."

"No, you're being hypervigilant like this is an active shooter game and a bad guy is going to pop up behind the wall and kill us."

"Don't even kid," Mel said.

"I'm not," Angie said. "You need to relax. Your anxiety is contagious and I'm already as twitchy as a cat in a room full of rockers trying to do this mom thing. Anxiety makes your mama's milk dry up, and I can't have that, and more importantly, Emari can't."

"Sorry," Mel said. "Maybe we should go inside."

"We're fine out here," Angie said. "Honestly, Uncle Stan has so many eyes trained on this house, no one is going to be able to get near it unless their DNA is one hundred percent DeLaura. Relax, drink your iced tea, and tell me why you look like you are about to start eating your own hair."

"I do not look like that," Mel protested.

"Yeah, you do," Angie said. "Good thing you wear it short."

Mel flopped back onto her poolside lounge chair. The April sun was warm on her face and she wished she were a cat like Captain Jack and her biggest concern was where she was going to catch her next four-hour nap.

"All right, there's been some difficulty at the bakery," she said.

Angie frowned. She reached for her unsweetened tea and took a sip. "Okay, I'm listening."

"I think we've been canceled," Mel said.

"What does that even mean?"

"It means that Nikki Guthrie has decided that we're a bad influence in Old Town and is trying to destroy our business by spreading the rumor that Naomi was shot because she was mistaken for me and it's cost us walk-in business and special orders."

"But we don't even know if that's true," Angie protested. "We don't know if there's a connection between the two shootings, do we? Has Uncle Stan found a connection? Why am I so out of the loop?"

"You're not. There's no connection that I know of," Mel said. "We're just two women who look a little bit alike who happen to have shops next to each other who were both shot at, one fatally." Mel's voice dropped an octave on that last bit. She still couldn't believe Naomi was gone.

Angie nodded. Then she narrowed her eyes and said, "What if everyone has it wrong?"

"What do you mean?"

"Because you were shot at first," Angie said, "we all assumed that the shooter came looking for you, maybe as revenge for some sleuthing you did in the past or perhaps to get even with your prosecutor husband, but what if it's neither of those things?"

"I'm sort of following you," Mel said. She sipped her tea before she continued. "If you could give me a little more direction?"

"What if the shooter was gunning for Naomi all along?" Angie asked. "What if Naomi was the target and we just assumed it was you because, well, you have a knack for getting involved in some seriously sketchy circumstances."

"For most of which you have been sleuthing right by my side." Mel felt the need to point out this little detail.

"True," Angie said. "But I wasn't shot at. In fact there's been no one coming after me at all, which makes me think it wasn't supposed to be you."

"Are you saying Naomi was the intended victim and not me?" Mel asked.

"Yes," Angie said. "I mean the backs of the bakery and the soap shop look identical, and you and Naomi are certainly a type, being tall with short hair and all. It could be that the gunman was looking for her and not you and got confused."

"But why?" Mel asked. "She's only been in business for six months and her shop is like ours, where the merchandise isn't hugely expensive and it's not like we deal with a lot of cash. Most people pay electronically these days."

"It might have nothing to do with robbing the business," Angie said. "What do we know about her personal life?"

"Not much," Mel said. "Married, no kids. I met her husband, David, once. He seemed nice enough. He sells men's suits, so he's not someone you'd think would have a lot of enemies."

"Yeah, an ill-fitting suit isn't really a reason to murder a man's wife," Angie said. "Unless the men's suit industry is a hotbed of violence of which I'm unaware."

"No, I think we can rule that out. Maybe it was personal. Dwight theorized that David was cheating on Naomi and his side piece got tired of waiting for him to leave her or maybe it was David himself."

"So, he hired someone to shoot her, or he shot her himself, or his girlfriend did?" Angie asked. "That feels extreme when you can just serve someone with divorce papers."

"Unless there was life insurance and he'd get a settlement."

"If he was in financial trouble, he might have seen it as his only way out." Angie tapped her chin with her forefinger. "I'd like to talk to him."

"You and me both, but Uncle Stan already waved me away. I don't see how we could make that happen given that we are under constant watch," Mel said. She glanced at the wall surrounding the yard. She couldn't see the security detail that had been hired but she knew they were there.

"I know. I feel like I'm fifteen," Angie said. "I appreciate the protection, especially for baby E, I do, but if I'm right and Naomi was the target all along, then all of this manpower to keep us safe is unnecessary and could be put to better use, like finding the shooter."

The back door to the house opened and the wail of a baby who needed her momma sounded like a car alarm on a loop.

"Angie!" A very harried-looking Tony stood in the doorway, holding a squalling Emari.

"Sorry," Angie said to Mel. "Duty calls."

"No prob."

Mel watched Angie head to the house and marveled that her best friend forever was now a mom. Angie had changed so much since Emari had arrived into the world. Everything about her seemed so different. She had more patience, smiles, and laughter, but she could also cut through the noise and chatter as if she'd achieved some sort of hyper focus. After all, she had made the insightful observation that Naomi might have been the target and not Mel. *Huh.*

Mel put a hand over her stomach. Was that what happened when a woman became a mom? They morphed into some multitasking idea person? Would that happen to her?

She moved her hand away. Although she and Joe weren't actively trying, they weren't not trying, either. They'd been married only a few months. They were still figuring each other out, mostly their cap-on and seat-down issues but as Mel gazed at the door she wondered, what would life be like with a baby on board?

Two o'clock in the morning was not Mel's favorite hour of the day unless she was unconscious and having a really good dream about chocolate buttercream or some other tasty confection. Any other interruption at that time was as unwanted as a case of fleas or a rejected credit card.

Because both she and Joe slept with their phones on their nightstands, it was doubly bad when both of their phones sounded off in the middle of the night. Usually, it was just Joe being woken up for some issue with a court case he was working.

Not tonight. Tonight, it was dueling ringtones. The Ramones' "Blitzkrieg Bop" for Mel versus Joe's old-school telephone bell tone. They both jolted awake, dislodging Peanut, who liked to sleep in between them, and scaring Captain Jack off the foot of the bed. He left with an indignant yowl as Joe snapped on the light on his nightstand and they both fumbled for their phones, trying to make the noise stop.

"Hello?" Mel answered.

"Hello?" Joe echoed.

"Mel, there's been another incident," Oz said.

"Situation?" Joe cried.

Mel frowned at him and plugged her free ear with her finger so she could focus on what Oz was saying.

"Oz, what are you talking about?" Mel said. She knew she sounded grumpy but in her defense she had been dead asleep and it was two in the morning.

"There's been another incident in Old Town," he said.

"When you say 'incident,' what do you mean?" she asked.

"Like with Naomi," he said.

"What?" Mel jolted upright. "Are you all right? Was it near the bakery? I'll come get you." She rose from the bed and headed for her closet.

"No, it wasn't near here," Oz said. "It was the guy over at the import store."

Mel froze. "Import? Do you mean Jacob Wright?"

At the same time, Joe said, "Jacob Wright."

Mel met his gaze and they both blinked as if they had no idea what to do with this information.

"There was another incident . . . situation," they said at the same time.

"Yeah, I know, that's why I called you," Oz said.

"No, sorry, I was talking to Joe," Mel said. "Is Jacob all right?"

"I don't know," Oz said. He sounded stressed. "Mick Donnelly stopped by and told me that something happened at Jacob's shop and the ambulance came for him but the area was cordoned off so he doesn't know if . . ."

His voice trailed off as if he couldn't make himself say that Jacob might have been killed.

"Oz, are you safe in your apartment?"

"No, I'm down in the bakery," he said. "When I heard all of the sirens, I figured I'd better come down and make sure the place was secure."

"All right," Mel said. "I'll be there in five minutes."

"You don't have to—" Oz began but Mel interrupted.

"Yes, I do," she said. "I want to make sure you're okay and find out what's going on."

"Okay, I'll hold the fort until you get here."

"Be safe."

"Always."

Mel ended the call and turned to Joe. She held up her phone and said, "Oz."

He tossed his onto the bed and said, "Ray."

"How did he hear about it?" Mel asked.

Joe shrugged. His gaze was somber when it met hers. "We're going to the bakery." He didn't say it as if it was a question.

"Yup."

"Let's go."

It took a few minutes to get dressed and give the pets treats so they would relax about this unexpected interruption of their nighttime routine. Joe drove Mel in his recently acquired SUV to the bakery while she debated whether she should call Tate and Angie. On the one hand, they'd want to know, but on the other hand the baby didn't give them a regular night's sleep these days and Mel really didn't want to wake them up if they were actually packing in some Z's.

They were halfway to the bakery when her phone rang.

"Hi, Uncle Stan," Mel said. She put it on speaker-phone.

"You heard," he said.

"I did," she said. "Oz called a few minutes ago."

"Is that Melanie?" Joyce asked in the background. "I want to speak with her."

There was a moment of silence in which Joyce had clearly won control of the phone.

"Sweetie," she said. One word and yet there was a truckload of meaning behind it.

"Hi, Mom."

"You're not going into Old Town on your own, are you?"

"Nope, Joe is with me." Mel smiled at Joe, who returned it while he sped through the empty streets.

"Dear Joe, well, all right, then," Joyce said. "Good night and be careful."

"Seriously?" Mel asked.

"What?" Joyce replied.

"What if I was going alone into Old Town?"

"Then I'd tell you to turn yourself around and go home."

"But because Joe is here it's all right?" Mel asked.

"Well, of course," Joyce said. "He's responsible and careful while you're . . ."

"I'm what?" Mel asked.

"Not so much."

"I think I'm offended."

"Oh, don't be," Joyce said. "I'm too tired for that."

Mel glanced at Joe to see if he was getting all of this. Judging by the grin he was struggling to suppress, he was.

"Well, don't let me keep you up," Mel said. "Can you give the phone back to Uncle Stan now?"

"Of course, love you," Joyce said.

"Love you, too, Mom."

"Hey, kid," Uncle Stan said. "I'll meet you at the bakery when I can. Do not go anywhere else."

"Where would I go?"

Silence greeted her question.

"I'm not going to the import store," she said.

"Good. There's nothing you can do there."

"Did they catch whoever did this?"

"I'm not talking about this with you."

"Why not?" Mel asked. "You know I'm just going to find out anyway."

"Maybe, but I'm not discussing an ongoing investigation," Uncle Stan said. "Your husband will back me on this."

Mel glanced at Joe and saw him nod.

"Fine. Check in when you can."

"I will," he said. "And, Mel, be careful. If there is a serial killer picking off random people in Old Town, you need to be on your guard."

"I will," she said. "And you be careful, too."

"Promise."

Mel ended the call and dropped the phone into her lap.

"You okay, cupcake?" Joe asked.

"I don't think so," she said. "I have a bad feeling that nothing is ever going to be the same again."

Mel and Joe arrived at the bakery in moments. They parked in front and used the customer entrance. The lights were on and Oz was sitting with two strangers at a small table.

Mel skidded to a stop, wondering if this was a hostage situation. Were these the serial killers? Had they busted in and forced Oz to . . .

She glanced at the table. There was a pile of cupcakes and a couple glasses of milk. The people, a couple actually, now that she noted the way the woman rested her head on the man's shoulder, looked wide-eyed and scared. The man was pale with a shock of red hair, which he wore short. He looked to be in his midtwenties. The woman also looked to be in her twenties with a deep brown complexion and long braids that reached halfway down her back.

Oz met Mel's gaze and shrugged. "I found the two of them hiding behind the dumpster when I took the trash out."

"Hiding?" Joe's voice came out strangled, as if he couldn't believe what he was hearing. He stared at the young people. "Who are you and what were you doing near our dumpster?"

Mel saw the woman flinch and she put her hand on Joe's arm.

"Easy," she said. "I think they were probably hiding because they saw something terrifying."

Joe glanced at the strangers and said, "Oh, sorry."

Oz gestured to the couple. "This is Payne and Karissa, they're tourists visiting from Virginia."

The couple gave Mel and Joe wan smiles.

"I'm Mel and this is Joe." They took the remaining

seats at the table. Mel noted that neither of them had eaten the cupcakes in front of them.

"If you try a bite, it might make you feel better," she said. "I know buttercream can usually fix whatever is ailing me, if only for a minute."

Karissa smiled at that and reached for the cupcake in front of her. It was a pistachio cupcake with a dark chocolate ganache. She took a tentative bite. The corners of her lips twitched and she let out a sigh, as if she'd been holding her breath for hours. She nudged Payne with her elbow and he picked up his cupcake. It was a chocolate cherry bomb with chocolate cake, cherry filling, and a tasty cherry buttercream. He took a bite and Mel watched his shoulders drop. No one spoke while they ate, giving them a minute to let all of the sugary, buttery goodness hit their bloodstreams.

"What scared you two so much?" Joe asked. He'd dialed back his prosecutor's voice and used his calmer, gentler, more reasonable tone.

"We were walking back to our hotel from a bar," Karissa said. She glanced at Payne.

He nodded. "And then we heard this horrible noise. We thought someone was in trouble so we followed the sound."

They glanced at each other as if reliving the moment.

Karissa continued, "We hurried around the side of the building, the import store, and we saw that the back door was open and the lights were on."

"So we went inside, thinking someone was hurt, and then we saw a man, lying on the floor," Payne said. "We went to check on him, but—"

"There was this weird flash," Karissa said. "Like lightning, except there was no storm, and then this person dressed completely in black . . ."

Mel sat up straight as if she'd been zapped. Karissa frowned.

"Sorry, go ahead," Mel said.

"This person all in black came running into the shop," Karissa concluded.

"It was scary and weird," Payne said. "So we booked it out of there and down the street and around the corner, where we called the police."

"So, why were you hiding by our dumpster?" Oz asked.

"We were afraid that the man in black saw us and would find us," Payne said. "We didn't know if we should go back to our hotel or not. Honestly, we were freaking out."

"Yeah." Karissa nodded.

"Would having the police escort you back to your hotel make you feel better?" Mel asked.

They nodded.

"Cool," she said. "We can help you with that."

Mel called Uncle Stan and he arrived in an unmarked car. He listened to what Payne and Karissa had to say and asked them if they'd be willing to stop at the station and fill out an official statement. The couple agreed and Mel packed up a four-pack of cupcakes for them to take with them.

As Uncle Stan was leaving, he hugged Mel and said, "Speak of this to no one. Tell the others."

Mel knew he wanted to keep what Payne and Karissa

had to say out of the local press. Another person dressed all in black had harmed someone. There was no word yet as to whether Jacob had survived the attack. Despite her recent cross words with him, Mel hoped with all that she had that the import store owner was okay.

Twelve

There was no news about Jacob Wright until later the next day. Much to the horror of everyone in Old Town, he hadn't recovered but had passed away from complications of a blunt trauma to the head.

Uncle Stan would neither confirm nor deny that the police believed that Jacob's death and Naomi's were related. In fact, he refused to talk about it at all, but Mel knew he suspected they were related because the security on the bakery and the staff hadn't diminished at all.

Mel spent the next few days in a flurry of baking, which seemed like a spectacular waste of time since there wasn't a customer to be found in all of Old Town. Even though the businesses were open, the entire district was like a ghost town and it wasn't just because of the incoming summer heat.

"Mel, you have to stop," Marty said. His voice was kind but firm. "There are no customers, literally none. What are we going to do with all of these cupcakes?"

Mel ignored him and continued piping fat swirls of mocha buttercream onto the tops of the chocolate cupcakes she had baked that morning.

"We can donate them to a food pantry," she said. "Or maybe we can take out the food truck and sell them in the park. I don't know. I just need to keep busy."

Marty took the pastry bag out of her hands and pushed her gently toward a stool. "Sit. I'll get you some coffee."

"I don't want—"

"You look like you're going to drop," he said. "Have some coffee."

"Okay," Mel relented. She rested her elbows on the table and propped her chin in her hands. "I don't know what to do, Marty. I feel as if everything we've worked for is going to be taken away and I don't know why or by whom."

Marty handed her a cup of coffee and Mel cradled it in her hands. The warmth from the cup felt like something tangible she could hold on to as it seeped into her fingers, and she suspected that he knew that.

"Thanks." She took a restorative sip and shifted her stool so there was room for him on the seat beside hers. She glanced up at him and said, "I'm scared."

"I know," he said. "And I know it's cold comfort but since Jacob Wright could in no way be mistaken for you, it does mean that if the two deaths were committed by the same killer, then the shooter wasn't after you specifically."

"Is it bad that I am relieved not to be responsible for Naomi's death?"

"You were never responsible, only the shooter can be held accountable," he said. "Don't forget that."

"I know," Mel said. "I just have so many questions and no answers."

"I think I know how we might be able to answer some of those questions."

Mel turned and faced the back door. Joe was standing there, looking devastatingly handsome, per usual, and it hit her square in the face that he was her husband, her partner, her best friend, and the person she loved most in the world.

Naturally, she reached for a cupcake and shoved it in her mouth to keep from letting all of the feelings she was having rush out of her in a gush of over-the-top goopy emotion. Because he was her soul mate he smiled and said, "I love you, too."

"Aw, that's sweet," Marty said. "Now how about we figure out what to do with all of these cupcakes?"

"I know what we can do with them," Joe said. "Half to the food pantry, for sure, but then we can offer the other half to Jacob Wright's widow as refreshments for the wake tonight."

"Refreshments?" Marty asked. "Are cupcakes normal at a wake?"

Joe shrugged. "Who knows? It's an excuse we can use to be there. Also, there's no body since he's still with the medical examiner, but apparently his mother is insisting on having a wake anyway."

"It must be so hard for her," Mel said. "But I don't

know if I can go in good conscience, knowing that the last words Jacob and I exchanged were in anger."

"I'll have Tate finesse it," Joe said.

"If anyone can, he can," Mel said. She bent down and retrieved some boxes from the cart under the table. She handed Marty a stack and said, "Get folding. We have deliveries to make."

Music played softly in the background of the funeral home. Mel stood beside Joe. He was in a charcoal gray suit and she was wearing a navy swing dress that was loose fitting but flattering to her tall frame. Mel had forbidden any of the brothers from coming as the last thing they needed was a scene but Uncle Stan and Tara were there and Mel knew that there were some plain-clothes police officers in the crowd as well.

A large framed photo of a grinning Jacob standing in the middle of his import store was on an easel at the front of the room. Instead of an open casket, the people in attendance were pausing and saying their final respects to the portrait and then giving their condolences to his wife, Kayleigh, who stood beside Jacob's picture, in a simple black dress with her thick blond hair pulled back in a soft knot at the nape of her neck. It was clear from her red eyes that she'd been crying and Mel felt terrible for her. Jacob had clearly been much older than Kayleigh and she was probably reeling from the unexpected loss.

Mel felt immense sympathy for the young woman.

She couldn't imagine how she'd handle it if she ever lost Joe, especially to an act of violence.

As they inched forward in the receiving line, she could hear the whispers in the crowd getting louder. She knew that some of the shopkeepers were talking about her. It was the same feeling she'd had when she was in school and the nasty whispers would start when she was called up to the whiteboard. Mel's love of pastry had not made adolescence easy, but if she could handle that then she could manage this now.

Mel kept her eyes forward and her chin level. She was not about to let them make her feel unwelcome or unwanted. She'd had nothing to do with Jacob's death and there was no way they could try and make a connection. There simply wasn't one.

"Hey, Mel, Joe, how are you?" Mick Donnelly greeted them as they moved up to where he was standing.

"Sad," Mel said. "Just terribly sad."

Mick hugged her and then turned to shake Joe's hand. "I know. I'm sure you would have liked the last time you saw him to be under better circumstances."

"Exactly," Mel said. "I mean, we knew each other for years and the only time we disagreed was that one night." She sighed. Her heart felt heavy just thinking about it.

"A relationship isn't defined by one moment," Mick said. "You know that."

"Yeah," Mel said. She nodded. "Thanks."

The line shuffled forward and Mel, with a little trepidation, approached Kayleigh. Did Kayleigh know how Jacob had felt about the bakery? Would she consider the donated cupcakes a gesture that was too little, too late by Mel? She reached back for Joe's hand and his fingers wrapped around hers with a reassuring squeeze.

Mel stopped before the portrait, waiting for her turn to speak to Kayleigh. Dozens of bouquets had been placed around the picture. The sickly sweet smell of so many flowers was almost overwhelming and Mel felt a bit nauseated by the onslaught.

She glanced at the portrait and sighed. "You'll be missed, Jacob." That was one thing she knew she could say for certain. Jacob had been a force of nature in Old Town and like him or not, his energy and drive were irreplaceable.

When the person ahead of her moved away, Mel approached Kayleigh. She'd met Jacob's wife at only a few of the monthly business association meetings and the annual holiday party. She was a very pleasant woman, always smiling and willing to help out in any way she could. Not today, however.

"Kayleigh, I'm so sorry," Mel said.

Kayleigh dabbed her face with a soggy tissue. She swallowed and glanced up at the ceiling as if trying to get her tears to spill back into her eyeballs. She blinked a few times and then lowered her head, sniffed, and said, "Thank you. And thank you for the cupcakes. That was very kind of you. Mocha chocolate was one of Jacob's"— *sob*—"favorites."

She began to tremble and when the tears came, they were unstoppable, streaking down her delicate face in a steady rain of pain. Mel opened her arms and Kayleigh stepped forward, letting Mel hug her.

"I don't know what I'm going to do without him,"

Kayleigh said. "He took care of everything, except he really didn't."

Mel patted her back and said, "Why don't you take a break from the line for a minute and get a cup of coffee?"

Kayleigh nodded. She turned to the woman on her other side and said, "I'll be right back, Louise."

Mel glanced at the stout woman dressed all in black; her face devoid of makeup, her wide nose, pointy chin, and haunted eyes were exactly like Jacob's. Judging by her age, she had to be his mother.

She waved a dismissive hand at Kayleigh and stepped into her spot by the portrait. Mel and Joe walked Kayleigh to a small alcove with a water fountain at the back of the main room. Joe went to fetch her some coffee from the refreshment room while Mel stayed with her, giving her a minute to catch her breath from her crying jag.

"I'm sorry," Kayleigh said. "It's been three days and I feel as if I should be accepting it by now but I'm not. I'm just stunned. I don't understand how this happened or why. I'm just . . ."

"I know," Mel said. "To lose Jacob like this, well, it's devastating. I don't know how you even begin to comprehend a loss like this."

"Exactly." Kayleigh began to sob again.

Mel grabbed a paper towel from a nearby dispenser and soaked it in cold water. She handed it to Kayleigh, who used it to mop up what remained of the makeup she'd been optimistically wearing.

"I'm going to have to sell the store," she said. "But who is going to want to buy a shop when the owner was beaten to death during a robbery?"

Mel went very still. While the rumors had been blazing through Old Town about the cause of Jacob's death, Uncle Stan had refused to tell Mel anything.

"It was a robbery?" Mel asked.

Kayleigh dabbed at her nose before she met Mel's gaze. "It would have to be, wouldn't it? Jacob was in the shop, doing inventory, he liked to do that late at night when he was all alone and couldn't be interrupted. I don't know if he forgot to lock the back door, or what, but it was unlocked and it appears the killer just walked right in."

Mel held her breath, saying nothing, hoping that Kayleigh would continue, while also feeling terrible about her unseemly interest in Jacob's death.

Kayleigh didn't continue so Mel asked, "Did they steal very much?"

"That's the crazy thing, other than whatever they used to hit him in the head, they didn't take anything," Kayleigh said. "I've been trying to go through the inventory to figure out what is missing. Jacob had a lot of fancy iron sculptures that he imported from South America and they found him on the floor in front of that display but I have yet to find one that's missing."

"Who found him?" Mel asked. She couldn't even pretend not to be gathering facts at this point.

"Some tourists were headed back to their hotel after a night out, and they heard a commotion," Kayleigh said. "When they went to investigate, the back door was open and . . ."

A sob cut off her words and Mel felt awful for pushing. "I'm sorry, I shouldn't have asked you about it."

"No, it's all right," Kayleigh said with a hiccup. "I don't have anyone to talk to and it helps me process it to say it all out loud. I just don't even know where to begin with selling the shop, our house, all of it."

Mel tried to think of something comforting to say. "It's too soon to make any major decisions like that. Give yourself some time."

"I wish I could but Jacob's accountant already told me that I'm going to have to liquidate everything and even then I might not break even," she said. "We have so much debt. I had no idea."

"Oh, no, I'm so sorry," Mel said. She suddenly flashed on how angry Jacob had been about her financial security. Clearly his anger had come from a place of fear. He must have known he was on the brink of disaster. "I don't want to pry but did Jacob have any life insurance? Maybe that could help you out."

Kayleigh shook her head. "He used it as collateral for a business loan from Business Equity Life. We're broke, broker than broke, we're in the negatives."

"Oh." Mel had no idea what to say.

Kayleigh dabbed at her face and then straightened her shoulders and let out a soft sigh. "Thank you for listening. Please keep this between us. I don't want the others to know. Jacob was so proud of his business."

"Of course," Mel said.

"Thank you," Kayleigh said. "For what it's worth, I think Nikki is wrong about you. You're not a spoiled little princess at all."

"Um, thanks," Mel said. She gave Kayleigh a small smile.

"I'd better get back out there or Louise will never stop berating me for being weak and selfish," Kayleigh said.

She heaved a sigh and Mel wished she could help Kayleigh with more than just a sympathetic ear and cupcakes but at the moment that was all she had to offer.

"If you ever need to talk again, please reach out," Mel said. "I'm always at the bakery."

"I will," Kayleigh said. "Thanks for coming today. I know Jacob wasn't very nice to you the last time you met. He hadn't been very nice to anyone lately."

"It's okay," Mel said. "He had a lot going on."

"Yeah." Kayleigh shook her head as if she still couldn't believe the free fall her life was in.

Joe arrived with a paper cup full of coffee and Kayleigh smiled at him in thanks. She turned and headed back into the main room, leaving Mel in the alcove with Joe.

"Is she all right?" he asked.

"No," Mel said. "But I'll tell you about it on the way home. Not here."

Joe nodded. He took her hand and led her through the crowd. They almost made it. Mel saw the exit just mere feet away. They were so close!

"What are you doing here?" Nikki Guthrie stepped into Joe's path, forcing them to stop.

"This isn't the time or the place," Joe said. He was using his prosecutor's voice and a normal person would have sensed danger and backed up. Not Nikki, however. He went to move around her but she wasn't having it.

"I'm not talking to you," Nikki said to him. She raised her voice and every person in the vicinity turned to see what drama was unfolding.

"Nikki, we're leaving," Mel said. "Step aside."

"Don't tell me what to do," Nikki snapped.

Mel wanted to loom over the shorter woman and bend her to her will. Instead, she thought about Jacob and his anger about his financial situation. She wondered if the reason Jacob and Nikki had been in such agreement was because she was feeling the same sort of stress. Mel tried to be understanding but her patience was about as thin as a runny ganache.

"Problem here?"

Mel glanced past Nikki to see Dwight, looking quite forbidding with his buzzed haircut and massive forearms crossed over his chest.

Nikki glanced behind her and her eyes went wide and then narrowed. "Oh, that's right, you're so special, you have your own entourage." She tossed her hair and very slowly, very purposefully stepped to the side, just barely.

Mel smiled at Dwight, who nodded at her and Joe as they left the room. When he fell into step beside her, Mel asked, "What are you doing here? I thought you were relieved from bodyguard duty when Joe was with me."

"I was in the neighborhood," he said.

"Convenient," Mel said. She glanced between the two men. She didn't believe for a hot minute that Dwight was in the neighborhood. She looked at Joe. "So, how long has he been tailing me?"

"He never stopped," Joe said.

"Ah." Mel nodded. "I should have known."

She glanced back at Dwight and gave him a considering look. "Octavius."

"Stop."

"Brutus."

"Have you got this covered?" Dwight asked Joe. He twirled his finger in the air, indicating Mel. "I've got a class to get to."

"I'm a *this*?" Mel asked. The men ignored her.

"Yeah, I'm good," Joe said. "But thanks for being around. I appreciate it."

They shook hands and Mel tried not to be put out that they treated her like something to be checked off a to-do list.

"What was that about?" Joe asked.

"I'm trying to guess his middle name."

"How about doing a search on the Internet?"

"Where's the fun in that?"

"Oh, of course. Where to now?" Joe asked.

"Back to the bakery," Mel said. "I need to talk to Tate. I'm hoping to have his financial brain explain a few things to me."

❧

Tate was waiting for them when they arrived. "How was the wake?"

"Sad," Mel said. "Aside from the absolute horror of Jacob being bludgeoned to death, it turns out he was in such deep debt that Kayleigh is going to lose everything."

Tate frowned. He was sitting at the worktable in the kitchen with a cup of coffee and a plate of cupcake crumbs in front of him. "Didn't he have life insurance?"

"Yes, he did and that's what I wanted to talk to you

about," Mel said. "Kayleigh said he used his life insurance as collateral for a small-business loan, but he was so deep in debt that she'll have to sell everything just to pay the debt off."

Tate whistled. "That's some really bad financial planning."

"But it's not uncommon to use insurance like that, is it?" Mel asked.

"No, not at all," Tate said. "A lot of people use their whole-life insurance as collateral."

Mel stared at him. "We haven't done that here, have we?"

"Uh, no," Tate said. "I would never."

Mel breathed a sigh of relief.

"Tate, have you ever heard of the company Business Equity Life?" Joe asked. "The name keeps popping up and I'm curious about whether they're on the up-and-up."

"I can look into it," Tate said. He took his phone out of his pocket and said, "I'll go make some calls." He headed into the office and closed the door behind him.

Mel and Joe exchanged a look. If anyone could tap into the financial questions surrounding Jacob's business, it was Tate.

Marty pushed through the kitchen doors with Madison right behind him.

"We're all closed up out front, boss," he said. He untied his apron and hung it on the hooks they kept on the wall for just that purpose.

"You know, Marty, you could be the face of Fairy Tale Cupcakes," Madison said. "You have a natural charm with the customers and the camera loves you."

Marty planted his hands on his hips and grinned. "Give this kid a raise. I like her."

Mel glanced at Madison and braced herself for the worst. "Has Marty gone viral?"

"Not yet," Madison said. She pocketed her phone and took off her apron, hanging it beside Marty's. Her shoulder-length honey-colored hair swished when she tossed her head and grinned at him. "But it's only a matter of time."

"But I don't want to get sick." Marty frowned.

"No, viral, not virus. Going viral is a good thing," Madison said. "It means you're super popular."

Marty looked at Mel and Joe in confusion. "These youths. It's like they don't want you to understand what they're talking about."

Mel laughed. She'd had her fair share of moments like that with Madison. The world was changing faster than she could keep up, which was why it was lovely to have Madison on board to navigate their online presence. She only hoped the social media maven could combat their current lack of customers with some snappy hashtags or something.

"I've told you, anytime you want me to give you a tutorial, I'm happy to," Madison said.

Marty shook his head. "Nope. When you get to be my age, life is too short to spend it with your nose pressed into your phone. I want to live every second I have to the fullest."

Mel frowned. Yes, Marty was in his eighties but he didn't usually talk about his impending demise. She wondered if Naomi's and Jacob's murders had bothered him more than she'd realized.

Madison grabbed her handbag from her locker and headed out the back door.

"Wait, I'll walk you to your car," Joe said.

"It's all right," Madison said. "My brother is parked right outside. He's picking me up because of the . . ."

"Murders," Mel finished for her.

"Yeah." Madison looked uncomfortable.

"If you ever don't want to come in, or if you want to take a leave of absence until the police have caught the person or persons responsible, that's fine with me," Mel said.

"Thanks," Madison said. "But I'm not worried. Both . . . incidents . . . were after the businesses had closed for the day and the victims were alone. I'm not planning to be either of those things."

"Still, you want to be very careful," Joe said. He escorted her out the door to her brother's car and then came back and sat down beside Mel.

"It feels different out there," he said. "It's not the happy, fun-loving Old Town we know and love."

"I know," Mel said. "And I'm afraid if they don't catch whoever did this, it never will be."

"They'll catch him," Marty said. "He's too sloppy not to get caught. I mean, he shot at you and missed, then he shot Naomi, and assuming it's the same person, he hit Jacob Wright with whatever was at hand. Why? Is he just wandering around town at night, looking for victims? There's no rhyme or reason to the killings. Clearly the guy is unhinged. If no one gives him an opportunity to strike again, he'll get desperate, do something stupid, and then they'll catch him."

"Which means no one is to be here alone, ever," Joe

Jenn McKinlay

said. Mel didn't think she was imagining that his words were directed at her.

"Okay." Tate popped out of the office. "Turns out Business Equity Life has been very busy in our little community and I have some information."

Thirteen

"Hit us." Joe perked up.

Marty plopped onto a stool and used his foot to push an empty one toward Tate.

Tate sat down and glanced at his phone, where he was reading something.

"Yes, Business Equity Life specializes in exactly what you were asking about," Tate said. "Business loans that use the borrower's life insurance as collateral."

"Which is normal," Mel said.

"Yes, it is, but in this case the interest rates are insane," Tate said. "I tapped some local contacts and found out that Jacob Wright had a loan at thirty-six percent."

Marty and Joe both made hisses of surprise. Mel blinked.

"Even to my math-impaired brain that seems awfully high," Mel said. "Is that legal?"

"It is," Tate said. He glanced up, his face scrunched up in thought. "It's a horrible rate set up to specifically prey on the most desperate businesses that can't get a loan through a bank or a more traditional lender, probably because of terrible credit."

"No wonder Jacob was so resentful of our financial stability," Mel said. "From what Kayleigh described, he was drowning in debt."

"He certainly was," Tate said. "This was clearly his last resort to keep his business afloat but how he thought he'd be able to pay it off, I can't imagine."

They were quiet for a moment. Mel wondered if everyone was thinking the same thing she was. When no one spoke, she finally broke the silence.

"I guess we know what we need to do," she said. All three of the men stared at her. "We need to approach Business Equity Life and apply for a loan."

\'\'\,\'\

"No, absolutely not," Joe said. This had become his refrain ever since Mel had floated the idea of applying for a loan from Business Equity Life two days ago.

"Why not?" she asked. "If there's a connection—"

"Exactly," he said. He turned the steering wheel and pulled into the first available space in the funeral home's lot. "If there's a connection, you're making yourself a prime target. Besides, there's no way that you can fake that you need a business loan. Your financials show that you're clearly doing well."

"Mom and Dad are fighting," Marty said to Oz in the backseat.

Mel whipped around to glare at him. "We are not fighting. We are merely having a difference of opinion."

"Sounds like a fight to me," Oz said. "Also, Joe's right."

"Dad's right," Marty corrected him.

"You are not too old to be put up for adoption," Mel said.

Marty grinned and Mel glanced at Joe, who appeared to be trying not to laugh. She crossed her arms over her chest. It was very annoying to have all three of them gang up on her.

Joe shut off the engine and said, "Come on. Let's just go to Jacob's funeral and see what we can find out."

"Do you really think his killer is going to stand up in the middle of a funeral service and admit to clobbering him?" Mel asked. She opened her door and slid out. She was trying not to be irritated but it was a struggle.

"No, but I think talking to friends and associates of his might give us some leads, you know, find out who else he was in debt to and that sort of thing," Joe said. He climbed out of his side of the car and met her gaze over the roof. "Listen, I know you want to find a tie-in to Naomi's shooting, but there might not be one."

"There has to be," she said. "You don't understand. I can't bear it if Naomi died because she was mistaken for me. It's eating me up inside."

Joe opened his mouth to speak and then closed it. Mel studied his face. Something wasn't right. He looked pained.

"What aren't you telling me?" she asked.

Joe met her gaze and his warm brown eyes were troubled. She'd never had him look at her this way before. Her newly acquired internal wife alarm started to clang.

"That's it!" Oz cried. He and Marty had also exited the car and he was standing beside Mel, staring at the car parked beside theirs.

"What's it?" Marty asked as he came around the back of the car.

"This car." Oz waved both of his hands at the car. "This is the car that the shooter drove off in that night at the bakery."

Joe hustled around the back of his car to join them. "Are you sure?"

"Positive," Oz said. "I remember the rims were custom, like these, with the *W* etched in the middle."

"Pretty sweet rims," Marty said. "That's an expensive car."

"Not really," Oz said. "Customizations don't always raise the value and this car is an older model. I'm guessing it's almost ten years old so not that expensive anymore but it was clearly someone's baby."

Mel glanced at the tires. They looked like regular tires to her but what did she know?

Joe walked past them and moved to look at the bumper. Mel followed him. Sure enough the license plate ended in N8. They turned to stare at each other with wide eyes.

"Wow," Mel said. She took a steadying breath and glanced at the funeral home. "That means the shooter's in there."

"So it would seem," Joe said. His brow furrowed in concentration.

Mel waited for him to meet her gaze. "What do we do? We can't go in there and we can't not go in there."

"If we don't go in there, someone else could get hurt," Marty said.

"Or not," Oz said. "If it's the same person who shot Naomi and bludgeoned Jacob, and it must be the same person because this is Jacob's funeral and this is the car that sped away from the bakery after shooting at Mel—"

"Breathe, Oz," Joe said. His voice was calm and Oz nodded and sucked in a breath.

"Thanks," he said.

"You're right," Joe said. "Given that this is the car you saw driving away and that this is Jacob's funeral, it ties the shooting and the murder together by potentially placing the shooter at the second victim's funeral," Joe said. "But we have no evidence that this car was in the area the night that Jacob was murdered. If this is a serial killer, however, it stands to reason that they're most likely here to savor the moment."

Mel shivered. She did not like this, not one little bit.

"Don't serial killers have the same method for their murders?" Marty asked. "Wouldn't it be weird that he shot at Mel, shot Naomi, and then bludgeoned Jacob?"

"Maybe Jacob got his gun away from him and he was forced to use something else," Mel said.

"Perhaps, but there's no way to know for certain until we catch them," Joe said. His face was grim. "For all we know, they have a grudge against Old Town business owners and they're about to go on a shooting spree. We need to evacuate the building immediately."

"How?" Mel asked. "What can we possibly say? That a cupcake baker and a district attorney think there might be a shooter in the middle of the funeral and you have to kick everyone out because of a partial license plate? How many license plates end in N8?"

"Well, when you put it like that, it sounds lame," Marty said.

"But the rims," Oz said. "Totally unique and I'm an eyewitness."

"You get back in the car." Joe pointed to Mel.

"What?" she cried. She spun on Oz and said, "You get in the car."

"Me? Why me?"

"Because you're the youngest," she said. "We need to protect you."

"I don't need you to protect me," he said.

"Cupcake, I'm not going to argue," Joe said.

"Good," she said. "Let's go. Oz, stay outside the building and out of sight. You, too, Marty."

Mel set off across the parking lot, leaving the three of them to follow.

"Damn it, Mel," Joe said. "Let's at least call Uncle Stan first. He can send some manpower over."

"Walk and talk," Mel said, holding her hand to her ear as if she were holding a phone. "We have no idea what this person's agenda is. You were right. We have to clear the building."

There were people scattered all over the grounds of the funeral home as they made their way into the building. Mel maneuvered around several of them but got held up in the doorway as a line had formed.

"I think we need to do the old someone-left-their-lights-on ploy," Mel said. "If we can get the funeral director to announce it, then we can see who goes out to the car and we'll have our shooter."

"Excellent plan," Joe said. "I just hope we can execute it in time."

"Really poor word choice, my dude," Oz said.

"Sorry," Joe said. "Of course, if the killer is the suspicious type, he'll know he didn't leave his lights on and probably won't fall for it."

Mel glanced at the two of them and then noticed that one of their party was missing. "Hey, where did Marty—"

That was all she got out before the sound of a fire alarm ripped through the building with all the subtlety of a high-speed train.

Mel clapped her hands over her ears.

"Oh, no, he didn't!" Joe yelled as the crowd pushed them back to the door.

Mel glanced down the hallway and saw Marty standing beside the fire alarm. He met her gaze and shot her a double thumbs-up.

"Yes, he did!" Oz shouted back.

The crowd moved en masse out of the building and back into the parking lot, forcing Mel and Joe and Oz ahead of them.

Marty elbowed his way through the crowd to reach them. "Pretty smart, right? I got everyone out."

"Subtle," Oz said. "Really subtle."

Marty frowned. "Just keep watch. When he goes to his car, we'll know who it is."

"I'm going to find a quiet spot to call Uncle Stan," Joe said. "Stay out of sight. Do *not* go near the car."

Mel, Marty, and Oz moved to the corner of the building, where they watched the crowd spread out in the parking lot. Mel spotted Kayleigh and her mother-in-law, Louise. Kayleigh was wearing a somber black dress with low-heeled shoes. Her eyes were red and she was dabbing her nose with a tissue. Mel couldn't see Louise's face as it was covered by a chin-length black veil. Very dramatic, but she had lost her son so Mel couldn't fault her.

Marty was scanning the crowd. Swiveling his head back and forth in an obvious way. Oz nudged him with an elbow. "Be cool. We don't want to draw attention to the fact that we're looking for the killer."

"Be cool?" Marty asked. He sounded outraged. "I am the definition of cool."

Mel met Oz's gaze over Marty's head and smiled. Marty was a lot of things but cool was not one of them. The sound of sirens grew louder as two fire trucks arrived on the scene. The crowd parted to give them room and everyone watched as the firemen headed into the building to assess the situation.

"Three o'clock," Marty said. "No! Don't look at the same time. Mel, you go first. Do you see him?"

"See who?"

"The guy," Marty said. "It's so obviously him. He's got *creeper* written all over him."

"Do you mean the man in the dark suit with the blue tie?" Mel asked. "That's not—"

"Yes, it is. Oz, take a look," Marty said. "I swear that's got to be him."

Oz glanced over. "The funeral director? You think Mr. Zimm is the shooter?"

"That's the funeral director?" Marty asked. He sounded appalled. "He looks like a criminal."

"The slicked-back hair is an unfortunate style choice," Mel agreed. "But I seriously doubt he's the shooter unless killing people is his way of drumming up business."

Both men turned to look at her as if she was onto something. She shook her head and they all went back to watching the crowd.

"Stan was inside, watching the crowd," Joe said as he joined them. "He's going to meet us over here."

"You didn't tell him I pulled the fire alarm, did you?" Marty asked.

"No, I think that's on a need-to-know basis."

Marty looked relieved and Mel looped her hand around Joe's elbow and pulled him close. She needed to feel his steadying presence. People were clustered in groups all around them and any one of them could be the owner of the car. What if they figured out they were being watched and panicked and decided to drive into the crowd? Mel felt her nerves wind tighter.

In minutes, Uncle Stan joined them outside. He glanced at the car and then at Oz. "You're sure?"

"Positive," Oz said. "Not only is the license plate a match but I remember the rims were custom, exactly like those, and it's a dark sedan."

"I'm going to talk to Mr. Zimm," Stan said. "The rest of you need to go. Now."

"We can't just leave," Mel argued. "It'll look weird if we do."

Uncle Stan frowned. "Kid, there is a possible murderer in attendance. No one is going back in the building. In fact, we're going to send everyone away for their own safety. That's why I need to talk to Mr. Zimm." He pointedly looked at Joe. "Get her out of here."

He turned to go back inside, but Oz gasped, drawing everyone's attention to him.

"It's Kayleigh Wright," Oz said. He pointed at the sedan. "She's going to *the car*."

They all turned to watch and, sure enough, Kayleigh, who appeared to be crying, was headed for the sedan. When she reached it and touched the door handle, the car automatically unlocked.

"It's her car!" Oz exclaimed. "That means she's the one who shot at Mel."

"Settle down," Uncle Stan said. "We don't have proof of anything."

"Well, if that isn't proof, I don't know what is," Marty said. "You need to nab her before she gets away."

Uncle Stan turned and gave them all a quelling look. "I'm going to go and talk to her. Do not interfere. Am I clear?"

They all nodded, although Marty looked reluctant to agree.

Uncle Stan strode across the parking lot, working his way through the guests who were being calmed by Mr. Zimm. The funeral director looked harried and Mel felt a pang of conscience that they had done this to him. She glanced back at Kayleigh. Oh, no, she had climbed into the driver's seat and appeared to be leaving.

The same thought must have occurred to the others as Marty cried, "She's getting away."

Joe had the keys to his SUV in hand and he bolted for his car, clearly planning to give chase if Kayleigh left.

"No, Joe, don't," Mel cried. "She could be dangerous." Although it felt ridiculous to say such a thing. She'd liked

Kayleigh when they spoke and the woman definitely did not give off the vibe of being a random serial killer.

"I'm just going to help Stan tail her if need be," he said. "Wait here."

Mel looked at Oz and Marty and said, "It's like he doesn't even know me."

She hurried after her husband with Marty and Oz falling in behind her.

"Kayleigh!" Uncle Stan called. "Mrs. Wright."

Kayleigh was either ignoring him or couldn't hear him because she didn't stop but rather kept inching her car out of its parking spot as she tried to ease her way through the throngs of people.

"Where is she going?" Oz demanded. "This is her husband's funeral. Is she just going to leave?"

"Looks like it," Marty said. "Human chain!"

"What?" Mel cried as she pushed through the crowd, trying not to lose Joe. "Excuse me, pardon me, coming through."

"We'll form a human chain," Marty said. "She can't drive over all of us."

"We're not doing that," Oz said. "If she's a murderer, she won't hesitate to run us over."

"Who's a murderer?" a voice in the crowd asked.

"Murderer!" another voice cried.

"Now you've done it," Marty said.

"What?" Oz asked. "You're the one who started it."

Kayleigh continued to back her car out of its spot. Uncle Stan was waving his arms, trying to get her attention. Joe hit the wrong button on his key fob and his car alarm started to go off. The crowd, already perturbed by the fire alarm, turned to look at Joe but he ducked into the driver's seat and avoided the condemning stares.

Uncle Stan whipped around and saw Mel and the others approaching. He raised his hands in the air in complete exasperation. "I told you to wait over there."

"But she's getting away!" Marty cried.

"No, she isn't," Uncle Stan said. He gestured to Joe, who had moved his SUV so that it blocked Kayleigh's exit.

"What is going on?" Kayleigh slammed out of her car. Her eyes were red and puffy. She sniffed and wiped her nose with the back of her hand. "I just want to leave." She glared at Joe where he was parked. "Get out of my way!"

She opened her purse and reached inside. Mel didn't pause to think it through or even to take a breath.

"No!" she cried. She leapt forward and slapped the handbag out of Kayleigh's hands, knocking it to the ground.

"What the he—!" Kayleigh shouted but Marty interrupted her.

"Arrest her, Stan!"

The crowd had gone silent, watching the drama unfold.

"Arrest me?" Kayleigh asked. She bent down to pick up her purse but Mel got there first.

"Not so fast!" Mel said. She opened Kayleigh's purse and reached in for the gun. Her hand closed around a phone. She shuffled her fingers around, grabbing a pack of tissues and a lipstick. That was it. Seriously? That was all she carried in her purse?

"Give me that!" Kayleigh demanded.

Mel turned away from her and thrust the bag at Stan. "Evidence."

"Of what?" Kayleigh cried. "That I wear lipstick?"

"No, that you're a murderer!" Marty announced.

"Are you all insane?" Kayleigh glanced from one face to another as if looking for their ringleader.

She looked so genuinely perplexed that Mel began to suspect that perhaps there'd been a mistake.

Fourteen

"Stop, everyone, stop." Uncle Stan's voice was fierce and they all froze.

Mel had heard him use that tone only the very few times when he was at his complete end.

"Mrs. Wright, I'd like you to come down to the station to answer a few questions," he said.

"Now?" she asked. "This is my husband's funeral."

"The timing is unfortunate but it's imperative that we do this immediately," he said.

"Do what?"

"Ask you why you're driving the shooter's car," Marty said. "The night shots were fired at Mel, the shooter drove off in that exact vehicle!"

A low murmur rippled through the crowd.

Uncle Stan whipped around and glared at Mel. "Muzzle him."

Mel looked at Oz and jerked her head in the direction of the SUV. Oz scooped Marty up by the arm and escorted him to the backseat passenger door that Joe held open.

"What's he talking about?" Kayleigh asked. "I don't understand. Why does that old man think my car had anything to do with a shooting?"

"I'll explain it all at the station," Uncle Stan said.

"No." Kayleigh shook her head. "Explain it now."

"A witness has placed that car at the scene of a shooting," Uncle Stan said. "So, we just want to get some information about the whereabouts of that car to clear it up."

Kayleigh looked at Mel. "Does he mean the shooting outside your bakery?"

Mel glanced at Stan but his face was inscrutable. She nodded.

"You think I shot at you?" Kayleigh asked. She looked as if she felt utterly betrayed and Mel felt a pang of guilt. How had this spun so out of control?

"No, I just . . ." Mel stammered.

"Why *did* you shoot at her?" Louise Wright appeared behind Uncle Stan. The people standing in the parking lot were watching with unabashed interest.

"Louise, I didn't!" Kayleigh hissed. "I've never shot a gun in my life! How could you say such a thing?"

"Well, that *is* your car," Louise said.

"It's not my car, it's Jacob's car. It's his pride and joy, the first car he ever bought new and even though it's ten years old he refused to get rid of it," Kayleigh said. "Mine is in the shop, and it has been for weeks. You know that."

"Yes, I do. Which makes this your car since it's the one you've been using." Louise sniffed as if as far as she was concerned, the matter was resolved.

Kayleigh's gaze flitted to all of the faces watching her. She looked scared, confused, and petrified. Mel didn't think she was a good-enough actress to be faking her fear and confusion and it was enough to convince Mel that Kayleigh knew nothing about the shooting.

"I need to get back to the service," Kayleigh said. She gestured to the funeral home. "I was only going to the Circle K to get a Diet Coke. I didn't have one this morning and I'm, well, I'm just not myself."

"We can get you one on the way to the station," Uncle Stan said.

"But what about Jacob's funeral?" Kayleigh asked.

"There's not going to be a funeral today," Uncle Stan said gently. "The firemen have to finish checking the building and the police do, too. It'll be a while before they let anyone in and by then most people will have left."

Kayleigh looked distraught. "But this was for Jacob."

"You can reschedule," Uncle Stan said.

"Typical," Louise muttered. "First you ruin his life, then you ruin his funeral."

She turned and walked away. It was an awful thing to say and Mel felt horrible for Kayleigh.

Tara Martinez arrived from amid the crowd. She took in the scene at a glance. She let loose a piercing whistle and twirled a finger in the air over her head.

"Move it out, people." Her voice did not invite debate

and the crowd loitering outside the funeral home started to walk toward their cars.

Tara's face was grim when she approached Uncle Stan and Kayleigh. "Mrs. Wright, I gave out my business card with my personal number at a recent Old Town business meeting. In clearing out the voice mail, I found one from your husband, left on the evening that he was murdered." She paused and made a pained face, which Mel took to mean she'd had an overabundance of messages and was annoyed that one from Jacob Wright had been lost in the onslaught. "He said he had something very urgent to speak to me about. Do you have any idea what that might have been about?"

"No, I don't, I swear." Kayleigh looked stricken.

"If you have an attorney, now would be a good time to call them," Uncle Stan said to Kayleigh.

"I didn't do it," Kayleigh protested. "I swear. I was going to leave him. Why would I murder him?"

Everyone grew silent at that. Kayleigh sobbed. Her voice was tiny when she said, "The night he was murdered, I had asked him for a divorce. He was so hurt, he left to go to his shop and do inventory, but then . . ."

Uncle Stan looked at her kindly but also gave no quarter. "Let's discuss this at the station."

The crowd watched as Uncle Stan and Tara led Kayleigh to his unmarked police car. They helped her into the backseat. Kayleigh looked shell-shocked. Mel felt her stomach twist. She simply did not believe that Kayleigh was the one who shot at her.

She took out her phone and sent an emergency text to a defense attorney she knew who she was confident would take the high-profile case in a heartbeat.

"Are you texting Steve Wolfmeier?" Joe asked.

"Maybe."

Joe stared at her.

"Probably."

He stared harder.

"Oh, all right, I am," she admitted. "If what she said is true, and I believe it is, that she was going to leave him, then Kayleigh needs help and he's the best. I'm sorry you two hated each other in law school but this is bigger than that."

"Actually, I was going to say I think that's a good call," Joe said.

"Oh." Mel thought there might be hope for her husband yet. "So, you agree?"

"Let's just say I find the situation odd," Joe said. "I can't see what motive Kayleigh or Jacob would have to shoot you or Naomi, so if Steve can help her that's a good thing."

"Exactly," Mel agreed. "There has to be some mistake. Why would Kayleigh have shot at me?"

"Maybe she confused you with Naomi," Oz said.

Mel thought about what Angie had said. It certainly seemed as if she'd been onto something.

"But why would Kayleigh have shot at Naomi?" Mel asked. "It doesn't make sense."

"Maybe Naomi was having an affair with Jacob," Marty said. His head was sticking out of the open window of Joe's car. "Maybe that's why Kayleigh asked for a divorce, but then in a fit of anger she clobbered Jacob, not intending to kill him but things go wrong sometimes."

"Maybe," Mel said. But she wasn't convinced.

The sound of the alarm stopped. The crowd stopped moving and watched as Uncle Stan drove Kayleigh out of the parking lot. Mel glanced at the funeral home, where Jacob's mother, Louise, stood on the front steps of the building, looking quite satisfied.

"But if Kayleigh is telling the truth and the car is Jacob's, doesn't that mean he was the shooter?" Mel asked.

She didn't add that Jacob had clearly had an issue with her. She didn't have to. Judging from the grim look on Joe's face, he was thinking the same thing.

"We're missing something," Joe said. "A big something."

"This is not like any memorial service I've ever been to." Lyn Anderson, the ceramicist, joined their small group. She studied Mel's face. "You okay?"

"Yeah," Mel said. "Whatever that is."

"Right?" Lyn was wearing a pretty blue head scarf that matched the color of the flowers on her dress. Her smile was sad when she added, "At this point, I feel like all we can do is try and stay alive."

Mel gave her a sideways hug and said, "Be careful out there."

"You, too." With a wave, Lyn departed.

They left the funeral home and drove to the bakery. Mel felt as if her brain were spinning. So much tragedy in so little time made her edgy. She glanced at the others and knew they felt the same.

They parked in the lot behind Fairy Tale Cupcakes and Oz left them to go to his apartment, while Marty headed into the bakery to see how Madison and Ray had done in their absence. Mel and Joe lingered outside, trying to process the events of the day.

"Should I call Uncle Stan?" Mel asked.

"No." Joe shook his head. "He won't be able to tell you anything even if he knows something, which I doubt he does."

"Because Kayleigh isn't the killer."

"I don't think so, no." Joe took her hand in his and walked her to the back door. "Are you going to be all right if I go into the office? I have some cases I need to follow up on. Dwight should be here in a few minutes. You can stay out of trouble for a few minutes, right?"

"I'll be fine," she said. She pointed to a car in the lot. "I believe that's one of Uncle Stan's undercovers."

Joe glanced at the car and smiled. "Looks like he's got it covered."

"I'd be lying if I said I wasn't relieved."

"Me, too."

He kissed her quick and headed back to his car. "I'll pick you up after work."

Mel nodded. She'd say it was overly protective on his part but she knew she'd feel the exact same way if the situation was reversed.

She opened the door to head inside when a movement caught her eye. The back door to Naomi's soap shop opened and her husband, David, stepped out onto the landing. Mel hesitated. Should she go over? She glanced at the parking lot but Joe was already gone. The under-cover officer was still in his car so she knew she was being watched. Surely, nothing bad could happen if she had eyes upon her at all times, right?

She let go of the doorknob and walked back down the stairs. It would be unconscionably rude not to give her condolences to David. In fact, her mother, Joyce, would be appalled if Mel, having seen the widower, did not go over and check on him.

David was stacking flattened boxes and didn't hear her approach. Mel's innate shyness kicked in and she wondered what she should say. Did she start with *hello* or jump right in with how sorry she was? Dilemma.

Before she could decide, David turned around and saw her. He jumped and Mel felt immediately awkward because she hadn't coughed or something.

"Hi, David," she said. "I'm Mel from next door."

He stood staring at her for a moment and then his gaze went to the bakery and then back to her. He was wearing navy blue slacks and a dress shirt but no jacket or tie. She wondered if this was his relaxed look.

"Hi," he said. His gaze bounced around the loading dock as if looking for a place to hide.

Mel wondered if she should have just left him alone.

"I'm sorry to bother you," she said. She moved to the base of the stairs and stared up at him. "I just wanted to tell you how sorry I am about Naomi. I didn't get to know her well, but I really liked her."

David nodded. He looked as if he'd rather be anywhere in the world other than here, talking to her. Mel understood. She'd felt the same way after her father died when people would tell her their favorite Charlie Cooper stories. On the one hand, she wanted to hear them, but on the other, it made the loss even more painful.

"Thank you," David said. "I don't . . . I just . . ."

Mel felt terrible. He looked completely undone and it wasn't like she knew him well enough to hug him.

"Naomi was such a talented soap maker," she said. "She gave me some bars that were inspired by my cupcakes."

David's lips ticked up on one side. "She sees . . . saw inspiration everywhere."

They were both quiet for a moment.

"Will you keep the shop open?" Mel asked.

David shook his head. "Uh . . . I can't. We hadn't even gotten to the profit-making stage yet and the place is hemorrhaging money."

His face crumpled and Mel didn't know what to say. To lose his wife and his business, the poor man.

"I wish I had the money to keep it open, but . . ." He shook his head.

Mel took a short breath. She didn't want to be rude, but she had to know. "Maybe there's a way. Our business manager, Tate Harper, might be able to help you. If there's life insurance or something . . ."

Yes, she was fishing. It was terrible of her, but it would be a connection.

"No, that's gone, too," David said. "She used her life insurance as collateral for the business."

"Oh."

"I told her it was a bad idea, but she was so determined to open her shop. We don't have kids, and this was her dream. I should have come up with a better way," he said. "Now it's all gone."

"Maybe if you explain the situation—"

David laughed but it was devoid of humor. "I tried talking to the owner at Business Equity Life, but he just wants his money. No excuses, no negotiations, no nothing."

Mel felt her entire body tighten. "Did you say Business Equity Life?"

"Yeah, when Naomi joined the Old Town Small Business Association, she asked John Billings who he recommended to help small businesses get start-up money and he recommended them," David said. "I should have known the whole thing was too good to be true. From the day we leased the building, everything that could go wrong did. We should have been able to pay that loan back no problem, but there were unexpected issues with the building and the money didn't go as far as we thought and then we couldn't make our payments. Honestly, the past six months have been a nightmare."

"Owning a business can be very unforgiving."

"Selling is our . . . my . . . only option," David said. He looked sick about it and Mel suspected that selling the shop on top of his grief was a double blow.

"If there's anything I can do," she said.

"Thank you. We'll, I mean, *I'll* survive."

Mel left him forlornly stacking the flattened boxes, wishing that a cupcake could make it better. For David, there weren't enough cupcakes in the world to help with the loss of his wife. Still, there had to be something she could do. She paused on the steps to her bakery. There was only one thing. She had to find Naomi's killer.

_/ ' _ ' _ \`

"I have some information," Mel said.

She and Joe had just arrived home and Mel had set to work making his favorite macaroni and cheese with ham and a side salad while he fed the pets. Captain Jack roused himself to partake while Peanut looked as if she'd been about to keel over dead from starvation. When Joe put her bowl down on the floor, she did her happy food dance, shifting on her front feet from left to right and then licking her chops before she slammed her face into the bowl. Not for the first time, Mel thought everyone should enjoy their food as much as Peanut did.

"Information?" Joe leaned against the counter and watched as she slid the homemade mac and cheese into the oven. "Interesting. Usually, you make my favorite meals when you're trying to *get* information."

"I do not," Mel protested. She absolutely did.

"So, if you're telling me you have information and you're still making my favorite, my deductive reasoning says that you are about to tell me something I don't want to hear."

"You think I'm buttering you up?"

He shrugged.

"I'm not." She set the timer on the oven. The man was too smart for his own good. She was going to have to be very careful with how she worded this. What had she been thinking when she married a prosecutor? The man was clearly too smart for *her* own good.

"Okay," he said. "What's the information?"

"Naomi's soap shop also had a business loan with Business Equity Life," she said.

"That's a connection to Jacob Wright."

"I think so," Mel said.

"How did you find out?"

"After you dropped me off, I saw David, Naomi's husband, out on the loading dock flattening boxes, so I went over to give him my condolences."

Joe glanced up at the ceiling as if praying for patience.

"I know, I know, I was supposed to go inside, but it would have been rude not to acknowledge his loss," Mel said.

"And if he was a murderer who shot his wife, how would that have played out?"

"He isn't."

"You don't know that."

Mel glanced at the oven. She really should have waited until he was eating before she said anything. Joe had a hard time eating and lecturing at the same time.

"I do know that," she said. "He also mentioned that the person who recommended Business Equity Life to them was John Billings."

Joe blinked. "Billings? With the mustache and the ten-gallon hat?"

"Yes, the same John who is the president of the Old Town Small Business Association," Mel confirmed.

"That's interesting."

"I thought so. David told me he is going to have to sell the business and hopes he breaks even. Naomi wanted the shop so badly that they took out a loan, using her life insurance as collateral but now without her, David can't keep the business open and he can't pay their loan so he's going to have to sell the shop just to be free of the debt."

"He told you all of that, huh?" Joe said. He looked unhappy.

"Yes, I thought you'd be pleased," she said. "This is important information. You don't look pleased."

Joe sighed and ran a hand over his face. "After dinner, we need to run an errand."

"What kind of errand?" she asked. Nothing about this

conversation had gone as she'd expected and she didn't like that one little bit.

"You'll see," he said. "But I'm going to need to fortify, so first we feast."

The oven timer went off and Mel went to grab her hot dish while Joe set the table. She watched him while they ate, trying to guess at the possible errand. He gave no hints but kept their conversation on neutral subjects like local sports and the weather. Mel listened intently for a clue as to where they were going, but he gave her nothing. Maddening.

After dinner, Joe excused himself to make some calls and he stepped out onto their backyard patio. Mel wondered whom he was calling. He paced back and forth. His square jaw was set and he looked tense. Finally, he ended the call and came back inside. Mel had been so restless while waiting that she did the dishes.

"Cupcake, you broke the unwritten rule," Joe said as he surveyed the kitchen.

"What's that?" she asked.

"That whoever cooks doesn't do the dishes," he said.

She glanced at the empty sink and listened to the gently running dishwasher. "You were busy and you were making me nervous. What's going on? Where are we going? Who were you talking to?"

"All in good time," he said. "I just want one promise before we go."

"Okay." Mel lifted an eyebrow.

"Promise you won't be mad."

"Mad? Why would I be mad?"

"A variety of reasons."

"That's not an answer," Mel said. "I'll have to take it under advisement."

Joe huffed out a laugh. "I can see I have been a terrible influence on you, Mrs. DeLaura."

And there it was, that disarming grin that got her insides all knotted up and got Joe out of trouble every single time. She refused to be weakened. Not this time. Not until she had all of the information. Otherwise, it would set a terrible precedent for their marriage.

They drove back to Old Town to the same condominium complex Mel had been hiding out in the week before. She studied her husband, trying to figure out what was happening, but he wasn't talking. To her surprise, Salazar and Margolis were there and they didn't seem equally as surprised to see her.

"Is Stan in there?" Joe asked Margolis.

"He just arrived."

"Stan?" Mel asked. She stopped walking and felt her heels dig into the carpeted hallway. "My Stan? Uncle Stan?"

"Yes," Joe said. "I had to loop him in to what you'd learned."

"Why?" Mel asked.

"You'll see," Joe said.

Mel rolled her eyes. "This is getting really old."

"Trust me," he said.

He held out his hand and Mel took it. He led her down the hallway, stopping outside a door about halfway to the end. He knocked in a weird rhythm, like a secret-code knock just like the one the undercover officer had worked out with Mel and Dwight. Mel frowned.

She heard someone at the door, probably checking the peephole. Then she heard the door being unlocked before it was pulled open. There stood Uncle Stan and behind him, visible on a hospital bed that took up most of the front room, was Naomi Sutter.

Fifteen

"Naomi?" Mel gasped. She blew past Uncle Stan and approached the woman on the bed. She appeared pale and weak but when she saw Mel her smile was warm and wide.

"Hey, Mel, fancy seeing you here." She reached out a hand and Mel took it in her own. Naomi's hand was cold to the touch and Mel wrapped it in both of hers as if she could give her some of her warmth.

"I thought you were . . ." Mel's voice cracked and she felt the tears well up in her eyes.

"Dead?" Naomi guessed. "Not for lack of trying on the shooter's part."

Mel thought her knees might buckle. Naomi was alive. She hadn't been murdered. But then why had Uncle

Stan told her otherwise? She shook her head. It was almost too much to take in. Why would he do that to her? The hurt was like a punch to the chest. She whirled around to face Joe and her uncle.

"Just to be clear—you knew," she said. "All this time I struggled and you knew she was alive."

They both looked decidedly uncomfortable. A depth of fury Mel did not know she possessed swept through her.

"How could you let me think she was dead?"

Joe said nothing, which was extremely unusual. He was the mediator, the negotiator, he always knew what to say.

"I only found out a few days ago. I'm sorry," he said. It was nowhere near enough.

"If you want to get technical, kid, I never told you Naomi had been killed," Uncle Stan said. "You assumed she had and I let you, which is actually what gave me the idea to let people think she'd died so we could keep her safe—it was touch and go there for a few days—and potentially flush out the killer."

"No! I don't want to hear it." Mel held up her hand in a stop gesture. She was not doing this right now. She turned back around to Naomi.

"I'll deal with them later," she said. She forced aside her hurt and anger and focused on her friend. She felt her throat get tight and she smiled through tears of relief and gratitude. "You're okay? Really okay?"

"I'm going to be," Naomi said. "I'm so sorry you were upset." Her free hand fluttered toward Uncle Stan and Joe. "They suffered for this decision but they had to do it to keep me safe."

"Save your strength," Mel said. "You don't need to

defend them. They made a decision and now they have to live with it."

Naomi glanced past Mel to look at Uncle Stan and Joe. There was a look of *I tried* on her face.

"I talked to David today," Mel said. "He knows?"

"Yes," Naomi said. "He was with me the entire time I was in the ICU."

"That explains why he was having such a hard time speaking to me," Mel said. "He kept saying *we* instead of *I* and everything was in the present tense and then he had to correct himself to the past tense."

"Poor guy," Naomi said. "He's certainly been through it."

"Is it true what he told me about Business Equity Life and that John Billings was the one who recommended the company?"

"Yes," Naomi said. "I heard about Jacob Wright. It sounds as if John was recommending that loan company to everyone."

Mel turned to look at Joe and Uncle Stan and, putting aside her hurt, she asked, "Do you think the loan company has something to do with Jacob's murder and Naomi getting shot?"

"It's the only thing they have in common other than owning a business in Old Town," Uncle Stan said. Mel nodded. If these two incidents were connected, the question became, Who was doing this and why?

"What else did Tate find out about Business Equity Life?" Mel asked.

"Not much more than he already told us," Joe said. "It's a small company that makes business loans at exorbitant interest rates to new or struggling businesses and it allows borrowers to use their life insurance as collateral."

"But Tate said that was fairly common," Mel said.

"It is," Joe said. "Except those interest rates are spectacularly high and given that opening a small business is a gamble to begin with, it cripples a lot of businesses before they get off the ground."

"Mindy Rios told me that a man named Dylan Lewis owns Business Equity Life," Mel said. "I'm assuming that's not an alias for John Billings?"

"No, it's not." Joe shook his head. "We've had both men under surveillance but so far there's no indication of any wrongdoing."

"And you couldn't have looped me in on this?" Mel asked. "So, this is why you de-escalated having Dwight be my bodyguard and why you let me out of the safe house. You knew I wasn't a target."

"We weren't sure of anything until Kayleigh told you about Jacob's debt and then Oz recognized the car from the night you were shot at in the parking lot at Jacob Wright's funeral, and even then we were trying to put the pieces together. Frankly, you weren't supposed to find out any of it," Uncle Stan said. "I didn't want you involved in any way until I could be certain it wasn't someone randomly targeting Old Town business owners."

"David is a terrible liar," Naomi said. "Sorry."

"Unlike some people." Mel sent Joe and Uncle Stan a dark look.

"Mel, I know you're upset, but your uncle suspected right after I was shot that whoever shot at you had mistaken you for me. I'm so sorry. If anything had happened to you because of me—"

Naomi's voice broke off and Mel patted her hand. Then in a voice loud enough for Joe and Uncle Stan to hear, she said, "I understand. It's a heck of a thing to think you might be responsible for someone's death."

"Cupcake—" Joe began but Mel interrupted with a shake of her head.

"Don't you 'cupcake' me," she said. "There is no excuse that I will accept that makes it okay that you let me think Naomi was dead."

"If I told you that I did it because the mere thought of anything happening to you destroyed me, would you forgive me then?" he asked. "We didn't know who the gunman was going for and we wanted to keep you safe. I love you, Mel, and I'd do anything to protect you."

Mel glared. She understood. She did. If she was in his shoes, she'd probably do the same, but she was not about to tell him that. Instead, she gave a hearty *harrumph* and turned back to Naomi.

"David said you have to sell the business, is that true?"

Naomi shifted against her pillows, trying to find a more comfortable position. "If I had died, it would be true because he wouldn't have been able to take over the shop and pay the loan, but I'm hoping with your uncle's help, we can find out who shot me and maybe it'll give us a chance to refinance our loan with another company without using my life insurance as collateral."

Mel turned to Uncle Stan. "Business Equity Life. You think they definitely have something to do with this?"

"Yes, and I think it ties Jacob Wright's murder with Naomi's shooting, since he, too, had a loan with them," he said.

"You're welcome for that information," Mel said. She paused to check her feelings. Yup, still mad.

Joe and Uncle Stan glanced down at the floor as if

duly shamed. The room was quiet and Mel waited a few beats before she spoke. She wanted to make certain her argument was airtight before she let it loose on them.

"Well, there's only one thing to do," she declared. "As I suggested before, Tate and I need to go undercover as potential borrowers—"

"What? No!" Joe protested. "That is absolutely not—"

Mel gave him a look and he stopped talking.

Uncle Stan looked at Mel, considering. She knew he was weighing the pros and cons and if she pushed for a specific outcome, he might refuse to listen to reason because he could be stubborn like that.

"Why Tate?" he asked.

"Because he understands finance speak, so he can likely make up a bogus business for us to present to the company."

"Given the recent shooting, don't you think the person at Business Equity Life will recognize you as the cupcake baker who was shot at?"

"We can wear disguises," Mel said.

Joe rolled his eyes. "I want to go on the record as not being okay with this."

Mel ignored him and looked at Uncle Stan. He met her gaze and then slowly nodded and said, "Call Tate."

"I never pictured you as a redhead," Tate said.

Mel flipped down the passenger-seat sun visor and studied her reflection in the tiny mirror. She didn't even recognize herself. A shoulder-length auburn wig, which was very itchy, false eyelashes, more makeup than she'd ever worn in her life, including a purple lipstick, and she was an entirely different person.

"I feel like I could flee the country and start all over and no one would ever find me," she said.

"Is that under consideration?" Tate asked.

"Maybe," she said. "I'm still mad at Joe."

Tate adjusted his fake, black-framed glasses on his nose as if he couldn't get used to them. Yes, this was the sum total of his disguise. Glasses.

"Nice specs," she said.

"Do I look smarter?"

Mel just looked at him. "How is a pair of glasses a disguise?"

"It worked for Clark Kent," he said.

"You're not Clark Kent."

"Neither was he," Tate said. "'I'm here to fight for truth, and justice, and the American way.'"

"*Superman*," Mel identified the movie quote. "And you're not Superman."

"You know Joe only kept you out of the loop to keep you safe," Tate said.

Mel knew that he and Joe had become the best of friends over the past few years and while she loved that her childhood bestie and her husband were close, she really felt his loyalties shouldn't be divided. Then again, Joe was also his brother-in-law so she supposed it was complicated.

Mel noticed that he'd angled his head down toward the tiny mic that was taped to his chest under his shirt as if to remind her that there were ears on them. She didn't care if everyone heard what she said. She was still mad at Joe and Uncle Stan and she wasn't going to pretend she wasn't.

"Blah, blah, blah. Are you saying you agree with what he did?" she asked.

"'Water bug! Not taking sides!'" Tate said. He raised his hands in the air quickly and then put them back on the steering wheel.

"*Bee Movie*," Mel said, identifying the movie quote.

"Nice." Tate grinned. "You're up on your animated films."

"I'm studying up for when we have movie nights with Emari," she said. "Which will not happen if you side with Joe on this. Now stop hiding behind movie references and answer me, do you agree with what he did?"

Tate sighed. "Of course I think he should have told you what was happening, but I also understand why he didn't. He's crazy about you."

"That doesn't make it okay."

"And if the situation were reversed?" Tate asked. "Would you withhold information from him if you thought it would keep him alive?"

"I am not engaging in hypotheticals."

"Good thing, because we're out of time," Tate said. He turned into the parking lot of an office complex. "We're here."

Mel glanced at the building. A sign reading *Business Equity Life* in blue script on a white background was attached to the side of the small, squat, stucco building. It looked very nondescript. It could have been anything from a dental office to a pawn shop. This did not instill Mel with a lot of confidence in the business loan company.

Tate checked his watch. "We're five minutes early. Do you want to go over anything?"

"Sure," Mel said. "My name is Suzanne Michaels and I want to open an antiques-and-collectibles shop in Old Town. I was referred to them by Naomi Sutter before she passed away."

"Perfect," Tate said. "It'll be interesting to see how Dylan Lewis reacts when you mention Naomi's name."

"Maybe. Uncle Stan said he has an airtight alibi for Naomi's shooting and Jacob's murder," Mel said. She shivered. It was still hard to believe that Jacob had been bludgeoned in his own store.

"That doesn't mean he's not involved," Tate said. "If this operation is like the mob, there are a lot of layers, like the associates, the soldiers, the capos, and the underboss, before you get to the power center, the boss, which makes them fairly untouchable."

"'Consigliere of mine, I think you should tell your Don what everyone seems to know,'" Mel quoted.

"Please." Tate rolled his eyes. "*The Godfather.*"

"Yeah, that was too easy," Mel agreed.

Tate checked his watch again. "Ready?"

Mel glanced at her reflection in the mirror one more time. Still unrecognizable, which gave her a burst of confidence that she could fool Dylan Lewis.

"Yeah, let's do this," she said.

Perhaps it was the talk of *The Godfather* before they entered or maybe Mel just had an overabundance of imagination but when the administrative assistant, a lovely young woman fresh out of college, ushered them into Dylan Lewis's office, Mel felt an acute pang of disappointment.

Dylan looked like every frat boy gone to seed that Mel had ever known. He was of medium height, sporting a belly and a thinning head of hair that he was trying to disguise with a spectacularly bad comb-over. He reeked of cheap cologne and his office was barren, as if it was temporary housing. None of it gave Mel a good feeling.

He was on his cell phone. "Of course, we're happy to lend a promising up-and-comer like you seventy-five thousand. I would consider it an excellent investment."

He glanced at Mel and Tate from where he was standing by the window and winked as if they were in on this deal with him. It was a smarmy wink, the sort a man who has just pocketed his wedding ring would give a single girl at a bar. *Ew.*

Dylan gestured for them to sit and Mel and Tate took the chairs across from his desk. They were utilitarian office chairs with black metal frames and thin cushions, the sort that made your butt go numb after fifteen minutes.

Mel glanced at Tate. She wondered how long Dylan would keep them waiting during his show. She had no proof, but her gut instinct was telling her that there wasn't anyone on the call with him. She sighed.

Dylan must have noticed her impatience as he made quick work of ending the call. How convenient.

Tate took point on the introductions. "Hi, Mr. Lewis, we spoke on the phone. I'm Pete Stevens and this is my partner, Suzanne Michaels."

"Of course, thanks for coming in. Call me Dylan."

He reached across the desk and shook both of their hands. Mel expected to receive a cold and clammy hand or a too-tight grip, but his handshake was solid. She bet he practiced that a lot.

"Now, the application you filled out online said that you wanted to open an antiques shop," he said.

"And collectibles," Mel added.

Dylan glanced at her and nodded with a frown. "What sort of collectibles?"

"Cookware," Mel answered at the same time Tate said, "Movie memorabilia."

Dylan glanced between them. "Sounds like you need to iron out some details there."

"It'll be both," Mel said quickly. "Cookware, movie memorabilia, anything from the '50s. The valley really owns the whole mid-century modern thing."

Dylan shrugged. "If you say so."

"We were referred to you by a friend of mine," Mel said.

Dylan glanced at her. "John Billings?"

"No," Tate said. He kept his face blank and Mel wondered if he was thinking the same thing she was, that it was interesting that Dylan just assumed John Billings was the one who referred them.

"Actually, it was Naomi Sutter," Mel said. "She owns . . . owned the soap store."

Dylan frowned. "Sorry, that name doesn't ring a bell."

"Really?" Tate asked. "She was just murdered. I'm surprised you don't remember her."

"Well, I . . . I have hundreds of clients," Dylan said. "I can't remember them all. I guess the name sort of sounds familiar. She was murdered, you say?"

"Yes." Tate's voice was cold and Mel nudged his foot

with hers to remind him to stay in character. "We didn't know her well, but it was still really sad."

"Yeah, that's too bad," Dylan agreed.

Knowing that Stan had interviewed Dylan enough to lock down an alibi for him, Mel thought it was really odd that he pretended not to remember Naomi. To what purpose?

Dylan studied the papers on his desk. Mel glanced at them and saw their bogus names on the top. "It says here that you're looking to borrow one hundred thousand?"

"That's right," Tate said.

"That's a lot of movie posters," Dylan said. He gazed at them with a calculating coldness in his eyes that Mel felt all the way to her spine. She could absolutely picture him, standing in the alley dressed all in black, shooting at a client so he could cash out the collateral on their debt. He was, quite simply, terrifying.

Mel felt her nerves kick in. Did he see through them? Her wig suddenly itched as if it were attached to her scalp with fire ants. She clasped her hands together to keep from scratching her head and risking a catastrophic wig loss.

"I think we can make this work," Dylan said. He shuffled the papers. "What do you have for collateral? Any business revenues?"

Tate and Mel exchanged a glance. This was the moment.

"We're a start-up, so no," Tate said. "But I sent in some profit projections with the application."

"Yeah, I saw those," Dylan said. His tone was dismissive. "But I'm going to need something more solid than future earnings. I have to know you've got something to offer if your business doesn't pay out. Any personal assets, like real estate?"

"I was hoping for a peer-to-peer loan," Tate said.

"Yeah, no." Dylan shook his head. "I can loan up to eighty percent of whatever collateral you have to offer, but it needs to be something I can actually liquidate to pay the loan in full if need be."

"We have our inventory," Tate said.

Mel gave him a side-eye. They didn't have any inventory! What was he doing?

Dylan wrinkled his nose as if he smelled something bad. "No, I don't want to have to sell antique cookware and movie junk. It has to be something that pays out immediately."

"I have a whole-life insurance policy," Mel said.

Dylan clapped his hands together. "Now we're cooking with gas. How much?"

"A quarter of a million," Mel said.

Dylan's eyebrows went up and then he smiled. "Excellent. Because you're a start-up, I'm going to cut you a break, the interest rate will be thirty-three percent."

"What?" Tate sputtered. "That's robbery!"

Mel snapped her head in his direction. She glanced at his face and it was clear the investment specialist in him had just taken over control of his brain.

"I think that's doable," she said.

"Doable?" Tate cried. "Do you realize how hideous that is? Assuming this is a fifteen-year loan, we'd be paying twenty-five hundred a month and in the end we'd pay three hundred and fifty thousand dollars just in interest! That's robbery."

Mel groaned. She was only surprised the mic strapped

to Tate's chest didn't catch on fire from Uncle Stan freaking out on the other end of it. This was not how this was supposed to go.

Dylan's face flushed red in anger. "Do you want the money or not?"

"Not!" Tate yelled. He hopped up from his seat and said, "Let's go, Mel."

"Mel? I thought your name was Suzanne?" Dylan asked. His eyes narrowed.

"It is," Mel said as she rose to her feet. "Mel's my nickname. It's short for . . . um . . . Mel . . . ancholy baby." She glanced at Tate. "Right?"

"Right, let's go," Tate said. "I'd rather sell my organs to a guy with a pickax and an ice chest than borrow from this guy."

"You do that!" Dylan yelled. "And I hope you get a staph infection."

"Still better than doing business with you," Tate snapped.

He took Mel's elbow and tugged her toward the door. He hustled her right past the administrative assistant and out into the parking lot.

Mel's phone started ringing immediately. She didn't have to look to know it was Uncle Stan. She let it go to voice mail. She could deal with only one outraged male at a time.

"What happened in there?" she asked as they got into the car and Tate gunned the engine and jetted out onto the street.

"I think I had a financial seizure," Tate said. He took several deep breaths, visibly trying to calm himself down. "Thirty-three percent? That's insane! I wouldn't take a loan from that guy if he was the only lender on the planet."

Mel waited a minute until his breathing appeared more normal. "You remember that we were supposed to go along with him and get a loan. Right, Pete?"

"Um."

"You might want to work on that response when you have to explain yourself to Uncle Stan."

"What was that you said about fleeing the country?"

"Not even that can save you now."

"Oh, boy."

Sixteen

"Well, that was a bust," Uncle Stan said. He glowered at Tate, who was sitting at the worktable in the bakery kitchen consoling himself with a banana dark chocolate cupcake. He'd said he needed the potassium. Mel thought he needed more than that but she knew better than to say it.

"I'll figure something out," Tate said. "On the upside, with the way he lied to us about remembering Naomi, we know there is something very sketchy about Dylan Lewis. I think it's worth following up with John Billings, especially since he just assumed it was John who sent us."

"Sketchy or not, we've had him under surveillance," Uncle Stan argued. "Nothing has come up. You were supposed to get inside, Tate. Argh."

Tate snatched a carrot cupcake off the tray Mel had put out and shoved the whole thing in his mouth.

"I'll figure something out," Tate insisted. "Just give me a minute."

"A minute is about all we have," Uncle Stan said.

Mel glanced at Joe. It was just the four of them in the kitchen, decompressing from the bust that was Mel and Tate's covert op. He met her gaze and asked, "Still mad at me?"

"No," she said. "Dylan Lewis, for all of his aged–frat boy appearance, scared the snot out of me. There was just something not right about him."

"What makes you say that?" Tate asked. "His lack of a moral compass in his willingness to rob people blind?"

"That and his eyes," Mel said. "He looked like a person who could absolutely murder someone for a nickel."

She shivered and moved to stand beside Joe. She put her arm around his waist. He looped his arm around her shoulders and pulled her in tight as if to reassure himself that she was okay.

"I, for one, am glad you freaked out, Tate," he said. "If that guy was giving Mel that bad of a feeling then I don't want us involved with him in any way, not even for a sham business loan to expose him."

Uncle Stan swallowed his cupcake and then cleared his throat. "Agreed. We'll find another way."

Tate visibly relaxed until Uncle Stan patted him on the shoulder, hard. "Nice effort, Harper, even if you did screw it all up."

"Thanks, I think," Tate said. His expression was bewildered so Mel pushed another cupcake at him and his attention was diverted.

Jenn McKinlay

"I'd better get back to the station and see if there's any other news," Uncle Stan said. He gave Mel one of his patent-worthy bear hugs. "Be careful out there, all of you. We still don't know who is responsible for the shooting next door or the murder of Jacob Wright."

"Is Kayleigh still under suspicion?" Mel asked.

"We're still trying to lock down her alibis for the night of the shooting and Jacob's murder," Uncle Stan said. He looked troubled.

"You don't think she did it," Mel said.

"Doesn't matter what I think," he replied. "I'm just seeking the facts."

With a wave, he left the bakery kitchen through the swinging door to the front of the shop. They all watched him go.

"None of this makes any sense," Mel said. "The only connection that Naomi and Jacob have is their loan from Dylan Lewis. While I can see him committing both crimes, Uncle Stan says his alibis check out. So, does he have associates?"

"If he does, there's no evidence of it," Joe said. "He hasn't met with anyone who would warrant a closer look."

They were all silent, pondering what to do next. When Tate spoke, his words came out slowly as if he was considering each one.

"We're going to have a meeting," he said.

"We are?" Mel asked.

"Yup." He nodded. His glanced up, his chin set at a stubborn angle and his voice determined. "We are going to find out exactly who has a loan with that shark, how deep they are in debt, and then we're going to figure out how to get them out of it. We may not be able to solve the murders but we are definitely going to ruin that guy's grift. Once we know who is in debt, we'll have another business owners' meeting and we'll invite Dylan Lewis to be the keynote speaker to his own takedown."

Mel and Joe exchanged a look.

"I like it," Mel said. Then she paused and added, "I like it a lot."

"Now, what's this about Harper?" John Billings asked. His mustache bristled when he spoke, the only indication that he might not be feeling as calm as he appeared. "I don't want to stand on ceremony, but I am the president of the business association and I'm usually the one to call the meetings."

The front of the cupcake bakery was packed with local business owners. Mel had been worried that, given the animosity some of the others felt toward the bakery, they might have a poor turnout but free cupcakes seemed to do the trick. Even Nikki Guthrie was in attendance and by Mel's count she'd already consumed two German chocolate cupcakes and was clearly eyeing a third.

Mel was relieved that the rest of the stress-baking she'd done was going to be consumed. Marty was hustling around the room with a coffeepot. The feeling that filled the room was one of curiosity.

"Sorry, John," Tate said. "I'm certainly not trying to usurp your role as president, but it's come to my attention that there's some hinky business dealings happening and I'm determined to get to the bottom of it."

John pushed his ten-gallon hat back on his forehead and studied Tate. "That is a concern. You should have come to me. Maybe I could offer some insight."

"I appreciate that, but I thought it best to have community input," he said. "I'm sure you agree."

Mel turned away to hide her smile. This was board-room Tate. No one in this room stood a chance against him.

"Of course," John said. It sounded forced as if he was sure of no such thing but had no idea how to disagree.

"Great," Tate said. He strode to the front of the room and faced the group. "Good evening, everyone. Thanks for coming on such short notice."

The low chatter in the room stopped as they all turned to face him.

"It has been brought to my attention that there is a bad element infiltrating the small businesses in Old Town," Tate began.

This was greeted by a boisterous rumbling in the crowd.

"By 'bad element' do you mean your bakery?" Nikki Guthrie asked. She sent Mel a dark look.

The room split right in half with some cheering her on while others protested the comment. Mel remained behind the counter with Dwight on one side of her and Oz on the other. Marty was in the crowd, holding the coffeepot and looking like he wanted to dump it all over Nikki. Mercifully, he restrained himself.

"I assume you're referring to the shooting that took place just outside our door?" Tate asked. "Seems to me that blaming the victim of the shooting is out of order, but I'm not here to debate that."

Anyone else would have looked duly chastened. Not Nikki. She tipped up her chin in defiance.

"What are you here to debate?" Clint Carlisle asked. He owned the exotic pet shop and Mel was relieved he hadn't brought his python to the meeting with him as he sometimes did.

"Not debate," Tate said. "I'm here to offer those of you who need it a way out."

"Out of what?" Nikki asked. She looked skeptical.

"Out of debt with Business Equity Life," Tate said.

Mel watched the crowd. Some looked startled while others were confused, but no one looked guilty.

"I recently discovered that there have been business loans given at exorbitant interest rates," he continued. "I'm here to offer my investment services to anyone who wants to get free from the crippling interest rates Business Equity Life offers."

"Your services?" Clint scoffed. "No thanks. I don't need some fancy business-speak from a guy born with a silver spoon in his mouth. Thanks but no thanks."

He sent Tate a look of disgust and strode to the door. The bells on the door handle clanged as he slammed it shut behind him. To Mel's dismay, several other business owners followed him. The room went silent in the wake of their departure.

"What exactly are you offering?" Nikki asked.

"I have pooled a group of investors who will buy up the loans from Business Equity Life and refinance them at much lower interest rates," Tate said. "If you're struggling to pay back your loans, this is a way to fix that."

"Well, now, I don't think—" John began to speak but was interrupted by a sob.

Everyone in the room turned to see Nikki, standing there with a cupcake in her fist and tears running down her face.

"Do you mean it?" she gasped. "Because I am about to lose everything, everything I've ever worked for, because I can't make my payments."

And just like that, Mel let go of all of her animosity toward the woman. The thought of losing her bakery because of financial distress made her feel every bit of Nikki's panic and fear and Mel couldn't help but empathize with her.

Nikki's confession opened a floodgate and several of the business owners who were in the same situation all began to talk at once. The picture they painted was one of financial desperation. It made Mel dislike Dylan Lewis even more for taking advantage of these people and their desire to live their dreams.

Tate began to take down names and monetary amounts, promising that he would do everything he could to help them. By the end of the meeting, they had a list of names and Mel felt as if the community she had always known, where the businesspeople helped one another, was on its way back.

When the last person left and they closed and locked the door, Mel collapsed against it in exhaustion. Tate was sitting at a table with Marty and Dwight and he rubbed his eyes as if he could wipe the tiredness away.

"We need to call Uncle Stan and give him this list of names," he said.

"What?" Mel asked. "Aren't we going to help them?"

"Of course we are," he said. "But first, we have to protect them. If Dylan Lewis does have associates who are doing his dirty work for him, then every single one of these people is in danger."

"You think he'd harm them to keep them from refinancing?" Dwight asked.

Tate shrugged. "I have no idea what the man is capable of but I wouldn't put anything past him when this much money is in play."

Mel felt slightly queasy at the thought, but she took out her phone and called her uncle to let him know what was happening. He arrived within ten minutes.

Marty and Dwight left for the evening, leaving Mel and Tate in Uncle Stan's care. The three of them moved to the kitchen, where Tate broke down the numbers for Uncle Stan, who let out a long, low whistle when he was finished.

"Nice work, Harper," Uncle Stan said. "And this time, I mean it."

Tate gave him a wan smile. "I'll take that as high praise."

"As you should," Uncle Stan said.

"What do we do now?" Mel asked.

"We don't do anything," Uncle Stan said. "I will make sure the district is under constant surveillance. Until we can tie Dylan Lewis to the murder of Jacob Wright or the shootings, we don't have anything."

"What can we do to help?" Mel asked.

"You can stay safe," Uncle Stan said.

"Aside from that," Mel said.

"Aside from that, you can let the police handle things," Uncle Stan said. He looked at Tate. "Back me up."

Tate looked at Mel. "He's right. We've done all we can do."

It didn't feel like enough to Mel but she knew they were right. Dylan Lewis was not a man to be crossed and by taking away so much of his income stream, he was going to be looking for retribution.

Business was slowly coming back to the bakery and Mel was so grateful that she didn't mind working late to finish up a special order. She wasn't alone because Dwight was here as Joe was stuck in his office working on a trial that was coming up.

Joe had insisted someone else could take over his case, but Mel drew a hard line. She was fine. He did not need to shadow her. Their compromise was that Dwight would be her buddy.

He had tracked down the last of the family and friends of the people who had been incarcerated because of Mel and everyone had an alibi that checked out for the night Mel was shot at. Now that she knew the person who had been gunning for her had likely mistaken her for Naomi, it was still a relief to know that it had not been her own actions that had brought about the shooting.

Mel would admit, only to herself, that Dwight was a reassuring presence, given that she had sent Marty, Madison, and Tate home at closing, and Oz was back at work at the resort.

Mel packed the last of the cupcakes into the walk-in cooler and cleaned up the kitchen. She had to work around Dwight, who was sitting at the steel worktable with his laptop open, studying for one of his cybersecurity classes. She watched him frown in concentration at his computer and she marveled, again, that her former high school nemesis was now her keeper. That was a life plot twist she never could have anticipated.

"All right," she said. "I'm finished. You are relieved from your duties as companion."

Dwight didn't glance up from his computer when he scoffed, "Companion? That makes me sound like a spinster in an Austen novel."

"You've read Jane Austen?" Mel almost keeled over.

"Saw the movies," he said. "On dates, not by choice."

Mel laughed. "But you actually paid attention to the plotlines."

Dwight shrugged. "Austen can deliver the snark like no one these days. You have to respect that."

Mel blinked at him. The man had layers, they were buried under smelly gym socks and a bad attitude, but he had layers nonetheless.

"Horatio," she said.

He slipped his laptop into his bag and shook his head.

"Give up. You're never going to guess it, DeLaura," he said.

"Balthazar," she countered. This time he laughed.

Mel checked the bakery one more time while Dwight packed up the rest of his things. They met up at the back door. Mel set the alarm as they stepped outside onto the landing. Dwight went first, surveying the alley before he waved Mel forward.

"Lee," she said.

Dwight's head whipped in her direction. He looked shocked.

Mel gasped. "That's it, isn't it? You're Dwight Lee Pickard."

"How did you guess?" he asked.

"I'm a genius, also I was running out of ideas." Mel did a little victory shimmy shake that made Dwight roll his eyes.

"Okay, genius, lock the door unless you want to stand here and be the bull's-eye in someone's target practice," he said.

Mel turned back to the door. She had just turned the key in the dead bolt when the sound of a gunshot followed by a bone-chilling scream ripped through the night air.

Mel and Dwight looked at each other and then he pushed her back toward the door. "Get back inside." He dropped his laptop bag at her feet and vaulted over the railing, running flat out in the direction of the scream.

Mel's fingers shook as she opened the door. She threw his bag and her purse inside and then pulled the door shut and locked it. Then she tore off after him.

Not being a runner, Mel got only halfway down the alley before she was panting for breath. She had to lean against the brick wall for a second and get her bearings. The sound of an engine revving caught her attention and she glanced up to see Millie Carpenter speeding by on her baby blue Vespa scooter. Mel recognized the helmet she wore as it had spikes on it.

What the heck? Was Millie the person who had screamed? Was she injured? She'd sped by too fast for Mel to see.

The sound of a siren wailing came from down the

street, so Mel began a light jog in that direction, keeping to the shadows as much as she could.

Brenda Jacobs, the tattooed sandwich shop owner, rounded the corner and slammed right into Mel, knocking her back a few paces.

"Brenda, what's—?"

"Run! They're going to kill us all!" Brenda screamed in Mel's face. Then she took off running in the same direction Millie had been going.

Mel disregarded the advice. She had to find Dwight and make sure he was okay. She followed the sound of the crowd. She found them easily, as there was a mob of people gathered in the street. Mel picked out Dwight's buzzed head right away as he stood a head taller than everyone else. She hurried to his side.

"What's happening?" she asked.

"What are you doing here?" he asked. He looked mystified. "I told you to wait inside."

She just stared at him.

"How does DeLaura put up with you?" he muttered.

"What happened?" Mel repeated her question.

"Someone shot the snake guy," he said. He gestured to the storefront. There were bullet holes in the glass. Mel's jaw dropped.

"Clint? Is he okay?"

"No idea."

Mel glanced at Millie's shop next door. She must have heard the gunfire and run for her life, which was why she'd zipped by on her scooter followed by Brenda, who owned the nearby sandwich shop. They must have been terrified. She glanced at Lyn Anderson's shop on the other side of Clint's and her heart dropped into her feet. There was a bullet hole in the window.

She clutched Dwight's arm and pointed. He glanced in the direction of the ceramicist's studio and uttered a curse. Then he began to shove his way through the crowd to the shop. The lights were on and he grabbed the door handle. It was unlocked. He pulled it open and Mel gasped. Lyn was lying on the floor in a pool of blood.

Seventeen

The next few moments were a blur. Mel and Dwight
dashed inside, dropping to their knees beside Lyn.

"Lyn, It's Mel."

Lyn was nonresponsive. She was lying on the floor,
bleeding from an apparent head injury, which had soaked
through the colorful green scarf she was wearing.

"We can't risk moving her," Dwight said. "Go get
help."

A crowd had gathered outside the door and Mel
pushed her way through, yelling, "Help! I need an ambulance."

Flashing lights showed that there was one parked
right in front of Clint's shop. Mel dashed to the vehicle.
Clint was sitting on the bumper while an EMT bandaged
his arm.

"Help! I need help," Mel cried. "A woman, she's bleeding and unconscious."

"Hey! They're taking care of me right now," Clint snapped.

"It's Lyn, next door, I think she's been shot," Mel said.

"I was shot, too," Clint protested.

"You were grazed," the EMT said. He patted Clint's shoulder and added, "You're good."

Then he and his partner grabbed their medical bags and took off running to tend to Lyn.

"Why are you here?" Clint yelled at Mel. "Did you do this?"

"What? No!" Mel said. "I heard a scream and I came to see—"

"Who got killed this time?" Clint sneered. "Ghoul."

"Shut up, Clint," Nikki Guthrie said. She pushed her way through the crowd. Her eyes were wide and her hands were shaking. She looked terrified. "Is Lyn all right?"

"I don't know," Mel said. She took a steadying breath and began to work her way back to Lyn's shop. Nikki fell in beside her.

"I knew someone else was going to die, I just knew it," Nikki muttered. A third EMT appeared with a stretcher. The crowd parted for him, and Mel and Nikki moved to the side of the front doors, trying to see but also keep out of the way.

Mel couldn't see anything except the backs of the medics, working desperately to save Lyn.

She glanced at the ground. Pottery shards littered the walkway, their turquoise hue shining in the light coming from the shop. It looked like someone had smashed a pot against the ground, but who? And why?

"Move aside, make way." Uncle Stan's distinctive bark drew Mel's attention. She stepped back into the shadows but without even looking at her, he said, "Don't bother, kid. You are in so much trouble right now."

Nikki glanced at Mel. "Your dad?"

"Bonus dad," Mel said. She saw Uncle Stan's lips twitch. He didn't smile but it appeared his ire had been put in park for the moment.

"What happened?" he asked.

"I was closing up the shop with Dwight and we heard a gunshot and then a scream," Mel said.

"I heard it, too," Nikki said. "But I heard several shots fired before the scream."

"Gunshots," Uncle Stan said with a glance at the bullet hole in the window.

"Dwight ran toward the noise and I followed," Mel said. "When we got here, we discovered Clint had been shot but then we saw the bullet hole in Lyn's window and we ran over. We found her on the floor. They're working on her now."

Uncle Stan nodded and then turned and went into the shop. Mel waited outside with the rest of the small-business owners. She glanced at Nikki, who still stood beside her, fretting her lip between her teeth.

"Thanks," Mel said. She jerked her head in the direction of the ambulance. "For backing me with Clint."

Nikki turned and faced her. "I owe you an apology. I met with Tate's investment team." Her voice broke but she forced the words out anyway. "It looks like I'll be able to get out of that horrible loan and be able to keep my store."

"Oh, Nikki, that's good news," Mel said.

"Yeah, I was so relieved," Nikki said. "Until this." She met Mel's gaze, her eyes dark with worry. "What's happening to Old Town?"

"I wish I knew," Mel said.

Just then the stretcher came out of Lyn's shop. She was still unconscious and the EMTs hustled her to the waiting ambulance. In moments, she was loaded inside and the vehicle whisked her away to the nearest hospital.

A pair of arms grabbed Mel from behind in a hug that almost knocked the wind out of her. She turned her head to see Joe. He had a look of relief on his face that made her heart stop. He pulled back and cupped her face in his hands.

"I had the police scanner on in the office. I heard shots were fired in Old Town and I about had a heart attack," he said. He kissed her hard on the mouth. "I've made up my mind. We're selling the bakery. It's too dangerous."

"What?" Mel asked. She caught a movement out of the corner of her eye. It was Nikki, shaking her head. Mel got the silent message. *Do not engage now.* "We'll discuss that later. Right now, I need to check on Dwight."

Mel sent Nikki a look of gratitude and then took Joe's hand and led him toward the entrance to the shop. Dwight was standing there with Uncle Stan.

"Is Lyn—?" Mel couldn't bear to say it out loud.

"No idea," Dwight said. "She didn't look good but they are taking her to the hospital so . . ." He shrugged.

Margolis and Salazar appeared out of the crowd. They waved Stan off to the side to talk.

"Did anyone see what happened?" Mel asked. She glanced around the crowd, looking for someone, anyone, who could tell her what went down.

"I haven't heard anything specific," Dwight said.

The police began to cordon off the area and their group was forced away from the shop front.

"As far as I can tell, someone shot at Clint and Lyn," Dwight said.

"Clint was one of the business owners who walked out of our meeting," Mel said. "But Lyn wasn't."

"We need to find out if they had any connection to Business Equity Life," Dwight said.

"No, no, we don't," Joe said. "This whole situation has gotten out of hand. I don't want any of our people to get anywhere near it."

"Joe," Mel said. She kept her voice soft as if she were talking him down from a ledge. "You know we can't do that."

"Yes, we can," he said. He turned on his heel and started walking. "See? It's so simple."

"That won't help us catch whoever is trying to kill off business owners in Old Town," Dwight said. "We have to find out who is behind it if we want to stop it."

"Or we could just close up the bakery and call it a day," Joe countered.

Dwight looked at him as if he was goofy. "Have you even met your wife? She's never going to let this go."

"He's right," Mel said. "Even if I closed the shop right this very minute, I'd still have to know who was doing this."

Joe looked pained.

"Lyn is my friend," Mel said.

"Mel! Joe! Dwight!" A shout interrupted whatever re-buttal Joe might have attempted. Tate came through the crowd, looking as harried as Joe had. "You're all right!"

"We're fine," Mel said. Tate crushed her in a hug and then did the same to Joe and Dwight, who looked ex-tremely uncomfortable, given that he wasn't a hugger.

"What happened?" Tate asked.

They recounted the events as best they could and Tate's face scrunched up in confusion. "None of this makes any sense. Lyn owns her shop outright. If our theory that Dylan Lewis is responsible for the murders because of the business loans he's made, Lyn proves that wrong. She owns the building her shop is in. That's why she can leave in the summer. She doesn't have a lease or rent or any business loan debt."

"Then we're back to our first theory," Joe said. "Which is that there's a serial killer in Old Town, which is why I think we need to sh—"

"Talk to Uncle Stan and see what he knows," Mel in-terrupted. She did not want to see Tate have a complete freak-out when Joe said he wanted to close the bakery.

They all glanced over at Uncle Stan, who was having a very intense conversation with the two officers, judging by the amount of hand gesturing that was going on.

"Maybe we should wait," Tate said.

"Agreed," Mel said.

It was the right call, as Uncle Stan and his officers began to clear the area to let the crime scene technicians in. Most of the crowd complied, except for Clint.

"You can't go in there," he said. He pointed to his shop as the crime scene crew stepped out of their van and headed for his front door. "My snakes are very sensitive. This sort of activity might put them off their food."

"You can stay here and let us go in or you can go wait in the jail. Your choice," Uncle Stan said.

Clint sat down on a bench on the sidewalk outside his shop. His arms were crossed over his chest and he looked furious. "I'll probably get shot out here."

"Then you might want to wait inside," Uncle Stan said through his teeth.

Clint pushed off the bench and headed inside, cradling his bandaged arm as if he were afraid it would fall off.

"He's a charmer," Dwight said.

"Only to snakes," Mel added.

✓⁄⸴ゝ⁄ヽ

"Has there been any word on Lyn?" Angie asked as she entered the bakery pushing Emari in a stroller.

"No, she's still unconscious, but what are you doing here?" Mel asked. "There's a potential serial shooter in Old Town. You shouldn't be out and about. You should be in your house or a vacation rental somewhere like Iceland."

Angie parked the stroller beside the worktable in the kitchen, except it wasn't a worktable at the moment. Instead, it was a book stand for Mel's collection of baking cookbooks, which she had scattered all over the surface while she studied recipes, because the brief surge of business that had come back had dried up again just as fast after last night's shooting. Mel figured it was as good a time as any to distract herself by crafting some new recipes.

"This place is surrounded by security and DeLauras," Angie said. "Emari and I couldn't be safer if we lived alone on the moon."

"Does Tate know you're here?" Mel asked.

"If we take out the human construct of time and look at it as being more fluid, then Tate knowing I was here later is really the same as him knowing I'm here right now, so in answer to your question, yes, at ten fifteen this morning, he knows."

"It's nine thirty," Mel said.

"Precisely," Angie agreed.

Mel could feel a headache coming on. "What happens at ten fifteen?"

"Tate will arrive from his office and you will tell him that it's time to have that business meeting with Dylan Lewis that he mentioned," Angie said.

Mel blinked. "Why would I do that?"

"Because it's the only way to get to the bottom of things," Angie said.

"How do you figure?" Mel asked.

Angie's face was set with a resolve Mel hadn't seen since Angie'd failed her driver's test twice and the third try was her last chance.

"Clint and Lyn's shooter has to be one of us," Angie said.

"When you say 'one of us,' who do you mean exactly?" Mel asked.

"One of the business owners in Old Town," Angie said.

Mel gave her a dubious look.

"Think about it," Angie said. "The targets of the murders or attempted murders have always been business owners. Not tourists, not random people on the street, but specifically people who own businesses in Old Town—Naomi, Jacob, Clint, Lyn, you—even if you were a mistake and we still don't know if you were or not."

"Okay, suppose that's true and someone is targeting business owners," Mel said. "I'm still not seeing how a meeting with Dylan Lewis and the business owners will help."

"Because who else knows the ins and outs of Old Town? Who knows the schedules of the local business owners, when they close their shops, when people work late? The only ones with that kind of information are other business owners," Angie concluded. "So the killer has to be one of us . . . er . . . them. So, if someone is working for Dylan as a hit man then it has to be one of the other business owners."

"Huh," Mel said. "That's some solid reasoning. And you came up with this when?"

"Three o'clock this morning while nursing the baby," she said. "I think sleep deprivation might bring out heretofore unknown levels of genius in me."

"That's one way to look at it," Mel said. "How exactly will we present this meeting?"

"Hang on," Angie said. She ducked her head into the stroller to adjust Emari's blanket. The baby was asleep with one chubby arm thrown up over her head. She looked like a partied-out rock star and Mel smiled.

"The point of the meeting will be to have everyone establish their alibis in public in front of witnesses," Angie said. "That's what hit me last night. That with so many local business owners arriving at the scene of the last shooting, it could be any one of us. So we have to figure out where every single business owner in Old Town was during the shooting of you and Naomi, the break-in and subsequent murder of Jacob Wright, and now the shooting of Clint and Lyn. It's the only way."

"I suppose. We need to ask John Billings to bring in Dylan Lewis, because I don't think he'd trust an invitation from anyone else. The few times I've run into John since Lyn was shot, I had the feeling he was trying to get away from me," Mel said.

"You and everyone else, according to Tate," Angie said. "John's staying off the grid, for sure. Don't worry, I think Tate can coerce John into bringing in Dylan. Tate's been looking at John's finances and he's not doing as well as he'd like everyone to think."

"Okay," Mel said. But it wasn't okay. She hated that everyone in Old Town was a suspect and she wondered if she'd ever feel at peace in her neighborhood again.

'\ '/ '\ '\

"I hope you know what you're doing, Harper," John Billings said. "There's enough happening in Old Town right now without you making it worse."

He lumbered down the sidewalk to Brenda Jacobs's sandwich shop with his boot heels clacking on the cement sidewalk and his overly large hat pushed back on his head.

"How could it possibly be worse?" Tate asked.

"Are you kidding?" John looked affronted. "It can

always be worse. What is it with you, Harper? Do you want to be president of the association or what?"

"What, definitely what," Tate said. "I told you why we're having a meeting and that Dylan Lewis needs to be in attendance. He's coming, right?"

"Yeah, he'll be here," John said. "I still say this is a job for the police."

"Oh, they're here, too," Mel said.

That seemed to give him pause, then he nodded. "Well, I can see you have it all in hand."

He pushed past them and into the shop. Mel had been shocked that Brenda had volunteered her space for the impromptu meeting, given that the last time she'd seen her, Brenda had been running for her life. She imagined Nikki had something to do with it, for which she was grateful.

A Porsche revved its engine and Mel glanced up to see Dylan Lewis parking his car in a space across the street. She felt her pulse pound in her neck. Would Dylan recognize her or Tate?

And if he did, would they be able to bluff their way out of it?

"Let me greet him," Dwight said. "He has no idea who I am. You two get inside and steer clear of him."

"Excellent plan," Tate said.

He turned and Mel was right behind him until a scooter cut off her route when it popped up onto the sidewalk. Millie Carpenter.

She switched off the engine, kicked down the stand, and pulled off her helmet. She plunked it onto the seat as she climbed off. She glanced at Mel.

"What's going on?" she asked.

Mel shrugged. She had decided that playing dumb was her best defense until Tate unleashed his plan to force alibis out of them.

She could feel Dylan getting closer with every step. She scooted around the Vespa and headed for the door. She noticed that the front fender was dented and she glanced at Millie and asked, "Were you in an accident?"

"Fender bender," Millie said. "A car didn't see me. Happens all the time. No big deal."

"No big deal?" Mel cried. She forgot all about Dylan. "You could have been killed."

"Well, I wasn't," Millie said. It was clear she didn't want to talk about it.

"Excuse me," a low voice spoke from behind Mel.

She knew that voice. Dylan Lewis. She froze, trying not to freak out. She kept her head down and stepped aside. "Sorry."

"No problem," he said. He began to walk past her and then stopped. He studied her face. "Do I know you?"

Mel cursed her short blond hair. The one time she needed to hide behind a curtain of hair and this thin, fine blond stuff was as useless as the fuzz on a duckling.

"I don't think so," she said.

"Huh." He continued to stare until Millie pushed past him and went inside. "Wait!"

Millie froze, looking terrified, but Dylan hadn't even looked at her. Instead, he snapped his fingers and pointed at Mel. "You're the cupcake baker. The one who got shot at."

Mel felt her spine relax. "Yup, that's me."

"I knew I recognized you," he said. "I never forget a

face." He dug around in his trouser pocket and took out a card. "I'm doing a Q and A on small-business loans in this meeting today. If you want some extra scratch, you should stick around. I can hook you up."

Mel took the card. "Thanks."

"Don't do it," Millie said. "You'd be better off giving up your firstborn."

Dylan turned to look at Millie. His smile didn't reach his eyes. "Millie Carpenter. Isn't this a surprise? Now, don't be bitter just because your cactus business is a bust."

"Succulents," she corrected him. "I deal in succulents."

"Well, you got the suck part right," Dylan said. With a mean laugh, he turned and went into the sandwich shop, calling over his shoulder to Mel, "We'll talk later."

Millie was so angry, she was practically vibrating but when Mel looked at her eyes, she could swear she saw fear in them.

Millie scurried into the meeting, leaving Mel on the sidewalk. She glanced back at Millie's Vespa and at the dent in the side. That was a weird place to get hit by a car. Mel studied the damage. It was circular, almost like a giant fist had punched the scooter. Mel leaned in. On the floorboard, wedged between the treads, was a bit of turquoise that twinkled in the sunlight.

Mel reached down and loosened it with her finger. It was oddly shaped and jagged. She flipped it over and realized it was a piece of pottery. It was from Lyn's shop and matched the shards that Mel had seen on the walkway in front of her store. How the heck had this gotten on Millie's scooter?

The answer clicked in Mel's mind like a light switch being snapped on. She pulled her phone out and called Joe.

"How soon can you get here? I know who shot at Clint and Lyn, killed Jacob Wright, and shot at Naomi and me."

Eighteen

Joe had already left work and was only a few minutes away. He parked down the street and jogged toward her.

"Okay, cupcake, you had me at 'I know,'" Joe said. "Tell me how? Or more accurately, who?"

They passed Dwight on their way into the sandwich shop, and Joe paused to lean close and say, "Keep an eye on the door. No one leaves."

"Got it," Dwight said.

Mel saw her uncle Stan across the eatery, standing with Brenda Jacobs, who looked about as terrified as she had on the night Clint and Lyn were shot. Nikki was beside her. Her narrowed gaze swept the room, landed on Dylan Lewis, and narrowed even further until her eyes were little more than slits. There was some righteous hatred there, for sure.

Tate was standing at the front of the room. If Dylan had made him, he didn't show it. Instead, he stood beside John Billings, smoothing his shirtfront as if awaiting his introduction.

The tables were full. Mel saw her friend Mick, and her non-friends Clint and Millie, and assorted other business owners. The missing ones were obvious, too, leaving empty seats where their larger-than-life personalities should have been. No Naomi, no Lyn, and no Jacob. Kayleigh was there, looking intensely uncomfortable, as any woman wrongly accused of her husband's murder would be. Mel was grateful to Steve, Kayleigh's attorney, who had convinced her to attend. He was sitting on her right, which Mel was grateful for as she suspected this was going to get intense.

Margolis and Salazar monitored the exits. It was, as they say, showtime.

"Thank you, everyone, for coming," Tate said.

"What are you doing, cupcake boy?" Clint asked. "John's in charge of this meeting."

"Actually, he's not," Tate said. "I called the meeting."

Surprised faces filled the room. Brenda turned to look at Nikki. Nikki didn't meet her gaze.

"Well, I'm not gonna sit here and listen to some stuffed shirt talk to me about running my business," Clint grumped.

"No, you're not, because I'm not here to talk business," Tate said. He paused. His face was flushed and it was clear he was holding on to his temper by a very frayed thread.

"That's right," Dylan Lewis said. "I am."

236

Several business owners in the crowd looked like they might be sick at this announcement—Clint was one of them. Mel noticed that most of the businesspeople squirmed in their seats and didn't look at Dylan, as if afraid he'd notice them.

Tate snapped his head in Lewis's direction. He frowned and said, "Actually, you're not. You're here because every bit of violence that has happened in Old Town is somehow related to you."

Dylan's eyebrows lifted and then his face turned an ugly mottled red. A pulse pounded in his temple. He crossed his arms over his chest and asked, "How do you figure?"

"Naomi Sutter had a loan with you, and she was shot," Tate said. "Jacob Wright also had a loan and was bludgeoned to death." He searched the crowd. "You were shot at, Clint. Let me take a wild guess here and say you have a loan with Business Equity Life, too."

Clint's mouth dropped open. Then he puffed up his chest and glowered at Tate. "That loan is none of your business, Harper. Besides, the person who shot at me was probably a serial killer targeting Old Town, otherwise why would they shoot Lyn? She owns her shop outright."

"A serial killer?" Tate asked. His gaze moved from Clint to Dylan. "Or an associate?"

"Associate?" Dylan balked. He raised his hands in the air with a fake laugh and said, "Yeah, like I'm the Godfather?"

"Exactly like that." Tate ground out the words and the room went still.

"Hey!" Dylan's gaze narrowed on Tate, sweeping over

him from head to toe. "I know you. You're the guy who came to me for a loan for a collectibles shop and freaked out when you found out what the interest rate was."

"More like robbery rate," Tate muttered.

"You don't want to pay it, don't borrow," Dylan retorted.

"Oh, I won't," Tate assured him.

They looked like they were about to take a swing at each other when the door opened and Naomi Sutter walked in on her husband's arm. The entire place went still.

Mel glanced at Joe and whispered, "I called her right after I spoke to you. I thought she'd want to be here for this."

"If I was her, I know I would," Joe said.

"Naomi! You're alive?" Nikki sputtered.

"I don't feel like it yet," Naomi joked. "But they tell me I'll survive."

Dylan glanced from Naomi to Kayleigh and the empty seat to her left where Jacob would have been sitting. It was all the confirmation that Mel needed. The final question in her mind was answered.

"Have a seat, Naomi, David," she said. She stepped forward and gave them both a half hug and then gestured to a table with two seats. "We were just about to get started."

"Started? With what? I thought I was here to look for new business. I'm leaving!" Dylan announced.

Tate looked like he wanted to tackle him, but Mel put her hand on his arm and held him back.

"I wouldn't do that if I were you, Mr. Lewis," Mel said. "Otherwise you'll never know who shot at me and

Naomi, who murdered Jacob Wright"—a collective gasp filled the room—"and who shot at Clint and Lyn."

"I don't care about any of that," Dylan said. "It's not my business if a serial shooter is on the loose."

"Given that you've invested in all of these small companies, I'd say it's very much your business," Mel countered. "I mean, I'm sure you want them all to be wildly successful so that they can pay their loans back on time?"

Dylan glanced away from her penetrating stare. "Whatever."

He strutted toward the front door. Two officers were there. He turned and headed for the side door. Two officers were there as well.

Dylan threw himself into an available chair and crossed his arms over his chest, looking like a petulant child.

"What's going on?" Tate muttered. "This isn't what we rehearsed."

"I know who the killer is," Mel said. "And the shooters."

"You do?" Tate gaped. Mel nodded. "Of course you do." He gave her a half bow. "Take it away, amateur sleuth."

"Hello, everyone, I'm Melanie DeLaura, part owner of Fairy Tale Cupcakes," Mel began because there were faces she didn't recognize. "I was the first person shot at in Old Town."

Several people nodded, remembering the night that started it all.

"At first, we thought that whoever had shot at me had an issue with me or maybe with someone with whom I'm close," Mel said. She didn't point out Joe or her uncle, not wanting to draw attention to them. "But then Naomi was shot. Please stand up, Naomi, if you don't mind."

With the help of her husband, Naomi stood up and Mel went to stand beside her. She glanced around the room, and said, "As you can see, we're a type."

Naomi smiled and so did Mel. Some of the people in attendance chuckled but others just looked confused.

"I assumed that Naomi was shot because she was mistaken for me," Mel said. "It tortured me for days and I was determined to find out who killed my friend because, much like all of you, I didn't know that Naomi had survived the gunshot."

Mel glanced at Dylan to see what he made of this. His features were schooled into a thoughtful look but Mel wasn't buying it. His eyes were wide and there was a sliver of fear revealed in the way he licked his lips like a nervous cat. They had surprised him with Naomi, just as Mel had hoped.

"I started to look for reasons why. Why Naomi and not me? Who had made such a grievous error?"

Mel began to pace the room. She felt her nerves flutter and a spasm of nausea almost brought her down. She did not like to be the center of attention and there were an awful lot of eyes on her. She could not get this wrong.

"Then Jacob Wright was bludgeoned to death in his own store," she continued. She glanced at Kayleigh, who looked like she might cry, and she felt terrible, but it was a part of the story. "Jacob did not look like me."

Kayleigh smiled and huffed a small laugh, which was what Mel had intended. Several other people smiled as well.

"It appeared Jacob was killed during a break-in but

they stole nothing. Why?" Mel asked. "Because they weren't there to rob the store, they were there to kill Jacob Wright."

Several cries of shock registered. Mel didn't look at Kayleigh, not wanting to see the widow's pain. Even if she had been planning to leave Jacob, losing him like that had to be awful, and what Mel had to say next was going to be devastating.

"It took me a while to put it together, the connection between Naomi and Jacob, but I finally did, and I realized that the person who shot Naomi was Jacob," Mel said.

Shock rippled through the room as the crowd reeled from the revelation. "His car was seen the night he shot at me, mistaking me for Naomi," Mel said.

She glanced at Naomi, whose already-pale face became positively pasty. Mel knew how it felt to think she was the cause of someone else being shot and she sent Naomi a sympathetic smile.

"But then Jacob was murdered," Mel said. "Why? What could have happened?"

Mel began to pace the room, meeting the gazes of the other business owners. Some glanced away but some met her stare with curiosity.

"With his business in deep financial distress and his wife about to leave him, Jacob had called and left a message with Detective Martinez, telling her he wanted to talk; he was murdered before he could. I believe Jacob wanted out from under whoever had ordered the hit on Naomi. He was going to confess, and he was murdered for it."

The tension in the room ratcheted up and Mel felt herself break into a sweat. She glanced at Uncle Stan and he gave her a small nod of encouragement. She couldn't look at Dylan Lewis. She was afraid of what she'd see, so she kept her gaze on the crowd.

"This leads us to the question: Who murdered Jacob Lewis?" Mel asked. "It was poorly done, a ham-fisted attempt to make it look like a robbery, clearly not the work of a professional."

She paced through the tables.

"No, Jacob's murder was done by someone who was also in serious financial trouble and about to lose everything, someone who thought that they could buy some time by doing the dirty work."

Again, she paused to let her eyes sweep around the room.

"The person who killed Jacob Wright was Clint Carlisle," she said.

"Lies!" Clint jumped to his feet. His face was red. His eyes darted to all of the exits, which were covered by the police. "This is the most ridiculous pack of lies! You're just guessing. You have no proof."

Mel took a deep breath. He was right, she had no evidence that he'd murdered Jacob. This was the shaky part of her theory but if she could bluff it out, maybe she could get a confession out of him. The entire room was a frenzy of whispers, but she shouted over them.

"Actually, I do have proof," she said. "But don't you want to know who shot at you, Clint? That person was sent to kill you for the same reason that Jacob was murdered, because you were worth more dead than alive and that person was trying to buy some time to pay off her debts just like you were."

Clint's head whipped from side to side, taking in

every person who sat in the room. "Who did it? Who shot at me?"

Mel felt every single person in the room look at her and she said, "Millie Carpenter."

Millie hunkered low in her seat, looking hunted. She didn't deny the accusation but just sat there in a scrunched-up ball of misery. Mel faced her and met the woman's trembling gaze.

"It was you, wasn't it, Millie?"

Millie didn't speak. She just shook her head in denial. Mel turned back to the room.

"Business Equity Life was the key," Mel said. "Each one of your businesses was failing. The only collateral you had was your life insurance. Tell them, Millie, tell them who ordered you to murder Clint to buy yourself some time to repay your loan and keep your shop open."

Millie's gaze darted to Dylan Lewis, but she pressed her lips together, refusing to speak.

"The night you were shot at, Clint, I heard a gunshot and then a scream," Mel said. "I assumed it was someone who'd heard the gunshots. It was."

The room went perfectly still. The crowd leaned forward as one, waiting for Mel to deliver her final piece of evidence, so she did. She pulled the pottery shard out of her pocket and held it up to the light. Its turquoise glaze shone brightly in the overhead fluorescent lights.

"I found this wedged in the footwell of your scooter. You weren't hit by a car, Millie," Mel said. "You were hit by a piece of pottery thrown at you by Lyn Anderson when she saw you trying to shoot Clint through the window, so you turned the gun on her and shot her, too."

A sob, which sounded as if it had been ripped out of

her, broke out of Millie and she collapsed into her chair and wept. Then she nodded.

"Who told you to kill Clint, Millie?" Mel asked. She kept her voice gentle, and pressed. "Is he in the room? Can you just point to him?"

Millie started shaking so violently her teeth began to chatter. She shook her head from side to side, clearly petrified. Mel felt her anxiety spike. If Millie didn't confess, this whole thing was going to blow up in her face.

Nineteen

"I've heard enough," Dylan said. He rose to his feet, the picture of calm. He smoothed his comb-over with one hand in a practiced gesture, as if he could control everything else if he could control his hair.

"'Not even close, bud,'" Mel said.

"*The Breakfast Club*," Tate said. Mel gave him a look and he dropped his head with a look of shame. "Sorry."

"The one thing I can't figure out is *why*," Mel continued. "Why was killing Naomi to get your hands on her life insurance your solution instead of just letting her default and then putting a lien on the business? Did you need the cash that badly and, if so, why?"

"I can answer that," Tara Martinez said. She looked at Uncle Stan, who nodded. "We found your storage unit, Dylan."

Dylan's face went red and then white and then red again. Whatever was in the storage unit scared him to death. Mel wondered if it was more bodies.

"Dirty, dirty money," Tara said. "You're going down, Lewis."

As one, the crowd looked from Dylan to Tara and back to Dylan.

"Eyah!" Dylan let out a panicked yell and ran full-out for the doors. He only got a couple of yards before Dwight appeared in front of him. He pivoted and bolted for the other door but Ray and Al DeLaura popped up in his way.

He spun again and made a straight dash for the window. He jumped into the air as if he planned to launch himself right through the plate glass.

Brenda let out a horrified shriek. "My window!"

Dylan never connected. Dwight made a flying tackle and brought him to the ground with a loud thump. The officers posted to watch the exits piled on and in a matter of moments Dylan was cuffed and hauled to his feet.

"You can't prove anything," he snarled. He yanked against the hands holding him. "I'll walk free and clear and you'll all look stupid. Do you know who I am?"

"Yes, I do!" Millie cried. She stood up, trembling but with a fierce glint in her eye. "You're the man who told me I had to shoot Clint Carlisle if I wanted to live." She slowly raised her hand and pointed a finger at Dylan. "It wasn't just to save my business. Dylan told me if I didn't shoot Clint, he'd kill me. He said Clint made a mess of everything with the way he killed Jacob and now I had to clean it up for him."

Millie looked at Clint with no regret. "I'd say I'm sorry but you did murder Jacob."

"Well, you shot at me and Lyn," he said. "And she might die."

There was a stir from the back of the room.

"I'm not going to die," Lyn said. She pushed out of the corner where she'd been standing in the shadows and walked carefully forward with her family circling her, preparing to catch her if need be. She wore a charcoal gray beanie with the edge of a bandage just visible beneath it. She looked pale and wan, but she was standing, looking like a warrior who'd arrived on the battlefield just in time.

Mel grinned at her, feeling her heart swell at the sight of her friend. Lyn smiled back.

"Sorry I was late to the meeting," she said. "I just woke up an hour ago. What Mel said was exactly right. I saw Millie shoot Clint through the window and I chucked one of my favorite pieces at her on her scooter, trying to stop her. Instead, she turned the gun on me so I ran back into my shop and closed the door. Glass does not stop bullets; in case you were wondering."

With that, her strength gave out and her family snatched her close and helped her into an available seat. She took a breath and looked at Millie. "I can't believe you shot me."

"I'm sorry. I do feel bad about that," Millie said. "I panicked." She looked wretched and walked over to Uncle Stan and held out her wrists. "Take me away."

Despite Millie's birdlike appearance, which usually garnered her automatic sympathy, there was no such feeling coming from Uncle Stan.

"Oh, I will," he said. He cuffed her. Millie deflated onto a nearby chair, like she'd been punctured with a pin. He jerked his chin at another officer, who cuffed Clint and forced him to sit in a seat next to Millie. They both turned away, refusing to look at each other.

The officers holding Dylan escorted him to the door. He made it as difficult as possible, thrashing and fighting all the way.

"You can't do this to me," he said.

"Weird, because we are," Salazar said.

Dylan went limp, dropping to the floor like a 180-pound sack of cement.

"Knock it off," Margolis said. "I will have no problem dragging you out of here by your feet."

Dylan was oblivious to her threats. He twisted around until he could see John Billings. "If I go down, you go down."

Billings pushed his overly large cowboy hat back on his head. He considered Lewis while he stroked his mustache. The normally affable expression that John wore vanished. He looked at Lewis with a chilling contempt that Mel felt all the way down to her toes.

"You better think about what you're saying," Billings said.

"Oh, I'm thinking," Dylan spat. "All of this was his idea, not mine."

Billings shook his head. "You can't touch me, Lewis."

"Can't I?" Dylan said. He struggled to his feet and Margolis and Salazar yanked him up by his elbows. "He's the one you want. Everything I've done, I did on his orders."

John huffed out a breath. He scanned the room, looking for allies. The crowd was too shocked to move. He smiled and spread his hands wide, looking very confident. "Clearly, he's trying to save himself by blaming me. Pathetic, really."

Mel thought about the business owners in Old Town and how John had recommended so many of them to Business Equity Life. They'd suspected he was getting a kickback, but maybe what Dylan was saying was true. Maybe the real mastermind behind all of the money laundering and murder had been John all along.

She thought about the hierarchy of the mob, which Tate had explained to her. If Dylan took his orders from John, then was there someone higher up than him or was he the main guy? How could they prove it? There were always layers of protection between the associates and the top man so that nothing would stick to the boss, but even Al Capone got caught with tax evasion.

Mel spun around and faced the room. "How many of you were encouraged by John to take loans with Business Equity Life?"

There was a beat of silence and then slowly hands began to rise in the air. There were a lot.

"That doesn't prove anything," John said. "I was taken in by Dylan, too. That's on me, but it doesn't mean I had anything to do with . . . whatever he was doing. I was just trying to help my fellow businesspeople out. I thought he was on the up-and-up."

"Then why did you come to the import store the night I murdered Jacob?" Clint asked. He sat glaring at John with a look of hatred that made Mel's toes curl. "Jacob was going to rat you out, too, and you needed him gone."

John's eyes went wide.

"That's right, I saw you," Clint said. "What's more, I have a picture of you."

"Impossible," John snapped. "I wasn't there. I have an alibi . . ."

Dylan began to laugh. He threw back his head in a cackle that resembled something a villain in a Marvel movie would make. "I'm your alibi, you idiot, or I was." He looked at Uncle Stan. "I lied. He wasn't with me the night Jacob Wright was murdered. He went to make certain Clint got the job done."

Billings balled his hands into fists. He looked like he wanted to charge Dylan. Instead, his gaze was penetrating when he looked at Clint and said, "You're mistaken."

"Nope," Clint said. "And I have the photo to prove it."

Mel gasped. "The lightning that the tourists, Payne and Karissa, saw the night of Jacob's murder. That was your flash."

Clint nodded. "That's right. Stupid cell phone." He glanced at John. "You've ruined my life and now I'm going to ruin yours."

Uncle Stan stepped forward. "Where is the photo?"

"I have it time-stamped and saved in several locations, and after I was shot at, I set it up so that if anything happens to me, it gets sent right to the police," Clint said. "Try and worm your way out of that."

Billings took a step forward, looking like he wanted to rip Clint apart but the officers intercepted him, cuffing his hands behind his back and leading him outside with the others. Mel watched as Millie, Clint, Dylan, and John were loaded into a waiting paddy wagon. It was going to be a busy day at the station.

With much murmuring, the rest of the business own-ers filed out, watching as the president of their associa-tion was hauled off to jail.

Uncle Stan walked over to Mel and held out his hand. She dropped the pottery shard into it. His fingers closed around it and said, "Nice work."

"You might have mentioned you were watching Lewis for money laundering," she said.

"It was just a hunch," he said. "Until we found his storage unit this morning."

"It makes sense," she said. "What else could he be doing? Clearly, whoever he's laundering money for is putting the squeeze on him to clean a lot of money and quickly. The only way he could do it was to invest in businesses that were sinking and have them clean the money for him, but even that wasn't enough so he had to start swapping out the dirty money with the life insur-ance payouts he was getting."

"So long as he and Billings are at odds, we should be able to get them to tell us everything," Joe said.

Mel turned to look at her husband. "Is this why you put me in the safe house? You knew there was something bigger happening?"

"Yeah," he said. He held open his arms and she stepped into them, hugging her man hard. "Sorry I couldn't bring you all the way in. It was too dangerous."

Mel nodded. "I can accept that but don't ever do it again."

"What happens now?"

Their phones went off simultaneously. Angie had posted a short video of Emari spitting carrots like a science fair volcano gone rogue to the group chat. Her message read: Now that I have your attention. What is happening?

Tate laughed at the video and said, "I think we need to do some cupcake recon at the bakery. I'll go fetch Angie and the baby."

"And I'll invite the rest of Old Town," Mel said. "We're going to need a new president of the business association and I think I know just the guy."

"No, don't even think it," Tate said. "I don't have the time or the interest."

*\ '\ *

"All those in favor of Tate Harper as the new president of the Old Town Small Business Association, say 'aye,'" Nikki Guthrie called out.

Every hand in the bakery shot up in the air. "Aye."

"And those opposed say 'nay,'" Nikki ordered.

Silence greeted this request.

"The *ayes* have it," she announced. She turned and clapped Tate on the back. "Congratulations."

The applause was thunderous and Tate looked equal parts pleased and resigned. The bakery crew stood in the corner, applauding their friend.

"For the record," Angie said, leaning close to Mel, "I am not calling him Mr. President."

"Obviously," Mel said. "It would cause a total power imbalance in the relationship unless you have him call you something more powerful, like 'Your Highness.'"

"Oh, I like that," Angie admitted. "I'll take it under advisement."

Mel laughed. Angie plopped Emari into Mel's arms while she went to hug her husband. Mel smiled as she watched her go. After the past few days of stress and anxiety, she finally felt as if Old Town was getting back to normal.

The baby started to fuss, so Mel took her out onto the front patio, where it was quieter. Emari settled down immediately, taking in the sights and sounds as she nestled against Mel's shoulder. Mel rested her cheek on the baby's downy head and watched the tourists wander by. The spring flowerpots were bursting with petunias and geraniums, the air was warm as summer was coming, and the shops were all open, looking normal for the first time in weeks.

Mel felt a surge of peace fill her up. Things were going to be okay. Tate would make an amazing association president, business would come flooding back, and they'd all chip in and help the businesses that were struggling. That was what made this district so special. They weren't just some bachelorette party destination, they were family.

The door opened behind her and Joe stepped out with Tate and Angie behind him. Marty and Oz followed them and the six of them stood, quietly appreciating that everything they had struggled to build over the years was going to survive and thrive.

Acknowledgments

First, I have to thank reader Lyn Andres-Anderson, who entered the contest to name the next Cupcake Bakery Mystery. Lucky for me, she came up with this spectacular title. It is absolutely one of my favorites. I hope you enjoy being a character in the story!

Many thanks to the amazing team that makes this series so special—Kate Seaver, Christina Hogrebe, Mary Geren, Dache Rogers, Jessica Mangicaro, Natalie Sellars, Christine Legon, Jennifer Lynes, Pam Burgoyne, Kristin del Rosario, and Judith Murello Lagerman. I feel so very fortunate to be surrounded by such talent and enthusiasm and I am ever grateful.

Finally, I want to thank my readers. Your support means everything to me and I look forward to writing many more stories for you in the future.

Recipes

Strawberry Surprise Cupcakes

A strawberry cupcake with chopped
strawberries inside and topped
with strawberry buttercream.

Strawberry Cupcakes

1²/₃ cups flour
¾ teaspoon baking powder
¼ teaspoon baking soda
¼ teaspoon salt
½ cup unsalted butter, softened

¾ cup granulated sugar
1 large egg
2 large egg whites
¼ cup buttermilk
⅓ cup strawberry puree
½ teaspoon vanilla extract
1¾ cup diced strawberries, set aside ¾ cup for filling

Preheat the oven to 350 degrees. Put 12 paper liners into a cupcake tin. Whisk the flour, baking powder, baking soda, and salt together. Set aside. In a large mixing bowl, whip the butter and granulated sugar until fluffy. Mix in the egg and then the egg whites. In a separate bowl, whisk together the buttermilk, strawberry puree, and vanilla extract. Alternately add the flour and buttermilk mixtures to the large mixing bowl with the butter, sugar, and eggs until just combined. Fold 1 cup of the diced strawberries into the batter. Scoop the batter into the cupcake pan, filling each one two-thirds full. Bake 20 to 24 minutes. Makes 12.

Strawberry Buttercream

½ cup strawberry puree
½ cup salted butter, room temperature
½ cup unsalted butter, room temperature
3 cups powdered sugar
½ teaspoon vanilla extract

In a small saucepan, heat the strawberry puree over medium-low heat, until it is reduced to 3 tablespoons. It takes about 15 minutes and will be thick. Pour into a small bowl (preferably glass) and put in the freezer to cool. This will take only a few minutes and it's good to stir it once or twice so that it cools evenly. In a medium bowl, whip the salted and unsalted butters until fluffy. Alternately mix in the powdered sugar, cooled strawberry puree, and vanilla until the frosting reaches the desired consistency.

Before frosting, I hollowed out the center of the cupcakes and scooped in the remaining diced strawberries. It kicks up the strawberry flavor and was a fun surprise in the cupcakes! When the cupcakes are cool, pipe the strawberry buttercream on top in the desired amount.

Vegan Coconut Cupcakes

A light, fluffy vegan coconut cupcake with vegan coconut buttercream.

Coconut Cupcakes

3½ cups all-purpose flour
1½ cups sugar
1 teaspoon salt
2 teaspoons baking soda
1 can full-fat coconut milk
⅔ cup coconut oil, softened
¼ cup water
2 tablespoons apple cider vinegar
1 teaspoon coconut extract

Preheat the oven to 350 degrees. Put 24 liners in cup-cake tins.

In a medium mixing bowl, combine the flour, sugar, salt, and baking soda. Whisk to combine. Next add the coconut milk, coconut oil, water, vinegar, and extract. Mix on medium-high speed with an electric mixer. Fill the cupcake liners two-thirds full. Bake for 14 to 17 minutes until the edges are golden brown and a toothpick inserted in the middle comes out clean. Let cool completely before frosting. Makes 24.

Vegan Coconut Buttercream

½ cup vegan butter or coconut oil
1 teaspoon coconut extract
5 cups powdered sugar
¼ cup water
Shredded coconut

In medium mixing bowl, using an electric mixer, cream together the butter and extract. (You can use softened solid coconut oil, but it tends to get runny, depending upon temperature.) Slowly add the powdered sugar until the frosting is thick. Then add the water a little bit at a time until you reach the desired consistency. You may not use all of it or you might want more. Top with shredded coconut.

Hummingbird Cupcakes

A moist cake made with banana,
pineapple, and pecans.

Hummingbird Cupcakes

3 ripe bananas
1½ cups all-purpose flour
¾ teaspoon baking soda
1 teaspoon ground cinnamon
¼ teaspoon salt
2 eggs
1 cup granulated sugar
½ cup vegetable oil
1 teaspoon vanilla extract
¾ cup canned crushed pineapple, drained
⅓ cup coarsely chopped pecans

Preheat the oven to 325 degrees. Put 12 liners in a cupcake tin. Using an electric mixer, puree the bananas in a small bowl and set aside. Using a medium bowl, whisk together the flour, baking soda, cinnamon, and salt. In a large bowl, using an electric mixer on medium speed, blend the eggs and sugar for 5 minutes, until creamy. Add the oil and vanilla, and mix for 2 more minutes until well combined. Slowly add the banana and pineapple, on low speed until just blended. Using a spatula, fold in the flour mixture until just combined, then fold in the pecans. Scoop the batter evenly into the cupcake liners. Bake for 23 to

27 minutes, until a toothpick inserted in the center comes out clean. Makes 12.

Cream Cheese Frosting

½ stick unsalted butter, slightly softened
3 cups powdered sugar
1 teaspoon vanilla extract
1 package cream cheese, room temperature

Using an electric mixer, beat the butter on medium until smooth. Add the sugar until the mixture has a crumbly texture. Add the vanilla and mix until fully incorporated. Mix the cream cheese in thirds, beating until just smooth. Makes 2 cups.

Gluten-Free Cupcake— Grapefruit Flavor with Chai Frosting

Grapefruit Cupcakes

¾ cup granulated sugar
1½ cups almond flour
1½ teaspoons baking powder
1 teaspoon vanilla extract
3 tablespoons grapefruit zest

3 tablespoons grapefruit juice
3 eggs, slightly beaten
½ cup sunflower oil

Preheat the oven to 350 degrees. Put 12 cupcake liners in a muffin pan and set aside. In a large bowl, whisk together the granulated sugar, almond flour, and baking powder. Create a well in the center and pour in the vanilla, zest, juice, eggs, and oil. Stir well until just combined. Fill the cupcake liners three-quarters full, and bake for 20 to 25 minutes, until golden on the edges and a toothpick inserted in the center comes out clean. Makes 12.

Chai Frosting

1 cup unsalted butter, softened
½ teaspoon ground cinnamon
½ teaspoon vanilla
¼ ground nutmeg
⅛ teaspoon cardamom
⅛ teaspoon sea salt
3 cups powdered sugar
4 tablespoons chai concentrate
2–3 tablespoons milk

With a mixer, cream all the ingredients except the powdered sugar, chai concentrate, and milk. Add the sugar 1 cup at a time, alternating with the chai concentrate and milk, until the mixture reaches the desired consistency. Makes 3 cups.

Turn the page for an exclusive look at Jenn McKinlay's next Library Lover's Mystery . . .

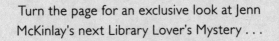

THE PLOT AND THE PENDULUM

Coming from Berkley in Fall 2022.

Lindsey Norris, director of the Briar Creek Public Library, was seated at the reference desk gazing out the window that overlooked the bay and the archipelago, called the Thumb Islands, within it. The large maple tree on the front lawn of the library was in its final stages of autumn vibrancy and the leaves were dropping like colorful confetti every time the ocean breeze stirred the tree's limbs.

October was here. For Lindsey this indicated that shorter days were coming, which meant winter would follow soon after with fires in the fireplace and days spent reading while the snow piled up outside. Bring it on.

She glanced around the library, watching the comings and goings of the patrons and staff. She liked to pause every now and then and try to see the library from a visitor's perspective. Was it engaging? Colorful displays of books greeted patrons when they first arrived and seasonal displays decorated the windows. Lindsey tried to change them out regularly to keep them interesting. Was the building clean? Yes, the town had an amazing cleaning crew and the staff made it a practice to sweep through and gather materials left on tables several times per day.

Was it friendly? Lindsey glanced at the first point of contact for patrons. The circulation desk.

Ms. Cole, the head of circulation, was stationed on the desk. She was wearing a white blouse with navy slacks in a shocking departure from her usual style of monochromatic dress in which she wore all shades of blue, whether they were complementary or not. Formerly, Ms. Cole had been nicknamed "the lemon" for her puckered personality, but she'd mellowed over the past few years and was presently running unopposed in next month's mayoral election.

Lindsey was resigned to losing Ms. Cole and despite the many ups and downs their relationship had endured since Lindsey's arrival, she found that she was going to miss Ms. Cole and her pragmatic ways. There was a steadfastness about Ms. Cole that was rare in employees these days.

Before she could get too maudlin, a scarecrow wandered past her desk, leaving a trail of leaves in its wake while a pack of children followed, collecting the leaves with the excitement only a group of toddlers could bring to such an activity. Lindsey met the scarecrow's gaze and he winked at her over the heads of the children.

Aidan Barker, the library's temporary story time person, was dressed in patched overalls that sported wide flannel pockets sewn onto his knees and bib, a flannel shirt, and a straw hat that was perched on his head. The kids gathered the leaves and raced back to him, stuffing his pockets until they were bursting.

A young boy who looked to be about three shoved a handful of leaves into one of the pockets on Aidan's knee, patted the flannel, and said, "Here's your insides, Mr. Scarecrow."

"Thank you, young man," the scarecrow said. Then he did a little jig as if adjusting his leaves. The boy laughed and scampered off to find more.

The child's mother smiled and said, "This is brilliant. Maybe I can get him to do some leaf pickup in our yard when we get home."

The scarecrow tipped his hat to her as she chased after her son.

Lindsey smiled and said, "Wild guess here. You're reading about scarecrows in story time?"

Aidan said, "Correct. We're reading *The Scarecrow's Hat*, *Scaredycrow*, and *Barn Dance!*"

"The kids will love it," she said.

"I hope so," he said. "My wife is a tough act to follow."

Aidan was the husband of Beth Barker, the library's regular children's librarian, who was out on an extended maternity leave with their newborn daughter Beverly, named for Beverly Cleary, the beloved children's book author. During Beth's final stages of delivery there had been some labor-induced talk of naming the baby Ramona or Beezus, but Aidan had prevailed and Beverly won out.

"How are Beth and the baby?" Lindsey asked. In addition to being her children's librarian, Beth was also Lindsey's best friend, and while they talked often, Lindsey had been giving the new mother some space, mostly to rest around the rigorous nursing and diaper-changing schedule she'd been maintaining for the past few months.

"Amazing," he said. "They're just amazing." His voice held a note of awe. "But Beth is ready to get back to the library. Thank you for arranging a job share so she can come back part-time. I don't think she'd be willing to leave baby Bee otherwise."

"I'm glad it worked out. And thank you for filling in for her story times. I don't think she'd trust anyone else," Lindsey said.

"Thankfully, my library director is a new parent, too," Aidan said. "She gets it."

Aidan was a children's librarian in a neighboring town, and he and Beth had met while doing dueling story times.

"Is there any chance we'll see Beth today for crafternoon?" Lindsey asked.

"She read this week's book, P. G. Wodehouse's *The Code of the Woosters*," he said. "So, she's planning to attend but it's really up to the baby."

Lindsey nodded.

"Mr. Scarecrow, can we have stories now?" a little girl asked. She had pigtails and was trailing a very grubby and clearly well-loved blanket behind her.

"Of course," he said. He shrugged at Lindsey. "Duty calls."

He clapped his hands in a short pattern and the children stopped what they were doing and clapped back.

And just like that, they gathered the last of the leaves and left the main area of the library and headed toward the story time room in the back.

The quiet that followed their departure was short lived.

"Hot dish. Hot dish. Coming through," a voice announced.

Lindsey turned to see Paula Turner walking through the main room of the library. She had two oven mitts on her hands and was cradling a casserole dish that was giving off steam. She was headed toward the meeting room where they held their weekly crafternoon sessions.

"Go ahead," Ann Marie Martin said as she joined Lindsey behind the desk. She was Lindsey's adult services librarian. Mother to two rambunctious tween boys, she considered this job her oasis from the chaos. "I've got the desk."

"Thanks. I don't have any questions to turn over to you. Other than a visit from a scarecrow, it's been very quiet."

"I'll take that as a good omen for getting my adult programming calendar done, then." Ann Marie smiled. Quiet moments in the library, which was the center of their small community, were rare.

Lindsey hopped up from her seat and hurried ahead of Paula to make certain the meeting room door was open for her.

"What is that?" Lindsey asked as she caught up to Paula. "It smells amazing."

"Sweet potato casserole with a crunchy pecan streusel," Paula said.

Lindsey opened the door and Paula entered the room.

The table where the crafternoon members gathered to discuss a book, work on a craft, and eat was fully loaded.

"You've been busy," Lindsey said.

"Don't tell the others, but you are my test subjects," Paula said. She put the casserole dish down on a trivet on the table and tossed her vibrant orange braid over her shoulder. Paula tended to dye her hair with the seasons or her mood, whichever motivated her the most when she was getting it done.

"Test subjects?" Lindsey asked. She wasn't sure she liked the sound of that.

"My parents are coming for Thanksgiving and my dad is a meat-and-potatoes guy," Paula explained. "I'm hoping I can serve a vegetarian meal and he won't be disappointed. So we have the casserole, figs in a blanket, salt-and-pepper radish chips, and cornbread, because cornbread goes with everything."

"Agreed." Lindsey nodded. "You're a braver woman than me. I would never subject anyone to my cooking by hosting a holiday meal."

Paula laughed. "Good thing your sister-in-law owns the Blue Anchor restaurant so you don't have to."

"I married up," Lindsey agreed.

She glanced out the window at the town pier, hoping to catch a glimpse of her husband, Mike Sullivan, known as Sully to his family and friends. He piloted the local water taxi that serviced the residents of the Thumb Islands and ran a seasonal tour boat as well. The pier was empty so she assumed he was out. This was another reason she enjoyed winter. More time with her husband as his tour schedule diminished.

"Are we late?" Violet La Rue asked as she and Nancy Peyton arrived.

Like the retired Broadway actress she was, Violet entered the room dramatically in her usual flowing caftan with her silver hair held back in a bun at the nape of her neck. With her deep-brown skin, large dark eyes, and prominent cheekbones, she was a strikingly handsome woman and people always turned to watch her when she crossed a room.

"We can't be. We're never late," Nancy Peyton said. Short with wavy hair that was slowly turning pure white and sparkling blue eyes, Nancy was a "Creeker," meaning she'd been born and raised in Briar Creek and had never left. Widowed young, she owned an old captain's house on the water, which she'd converted into three apartments, one of which Lindsey had lived in when she first arrived in town.

While technically senior citizens, both Nancy and Violet were incredibly active in the community. They were also two of Lindsey's favorite residents and had been with the crafternoon club since the beginning.

Lindsey noticed that they both carried their crochet bags. She sighed. The only part of crafternoon that she didn't care for was the craft part. She was equally awful at all crafts and no matter what she tried she just couldn't craft to save her life. Recently, they'd been working on crocheting bucket hats. It was excruciating.

"Where's your project?" Paula asked, looking pointedly at Lindsey's empty hands.

"Did you know Sir Pelham Grenville Wodehouse was called 'Plum' by his friends and family?" Lindsey asked.

"She's changing the subject," Nancy said to the others. "That means she's made a muddle of her crochet."

"Who made a muddle of their crochet?" a voice asked. They all turned to the door to see Beth arrive, pushing a stroller.

"Baby Bee is here," Nancy cried, keeping her voice soft in case the baby was sleeping.

Any talk of crochet was forgotten as they all gathered around to admire the baby, for which Lindsey was grateful. She really didn't want to trot out the tangle of yarn that was supposed to be a hat in front of her friends. She joined the group as they gazed in wonder at Beth's little girl.

At five months old, Bee was a pudgy butterball of unparalleled cuteness. She had her mother's dark hair and pert nose and her father's dimpled chin and pretty eyes. She blinked up at them, not at all alarmed to have so many faces peering down at her.

Beth unfastened the strap that held her in and hefted her out of the stroller. Nancy was there with her arms outstretched and Beth handed her over, clearly happy to share. Bee gurgled at Nancy, who looked enchanted.

Beth stretched and sat on one of the sofas in the room, looking relieved to have a rest for a minute. Nancy walked the baby about the room with Violet by her side.

"I knew it was a genius idea to read this week's book," Beth said. "Now I can sit here and eat lunch without interruption for the first time in months."

"I hope you like sweet potatoes," Paula said.

"Love them," Beth assured her.

"Lindsey, there's a man waiting out in the lobby for

you," Ms. Cole said as she entered the room, clutching her crochet bag and a copy of this week's book.

"Oh?" Lindsey asked. Ms. Cole appeared agitated, which was unusual for the normally unflappable librarian.

"I would have sent him away but I believe he's *William Dorchester*," Ms. Cole explained in a hushed tone.

Nancy gasped. Her eyes were wide and stared at Ms. Cole as if she couldn't believe what she'd just heard.

The rest of the crafternooners glanced between the two women. Violet took the opportunity to lift the baby from Nancy's arms and it showed how distracted Nancy was that she let her.

"Are you sure?" Nancy asked Ms. Cole.

"Not one hundred percent," Ms. Cole admitted. "I tried to get his name but he said he preferred not to give it."

"That's weird," Paula said.

Lindsey silently agreed.

"Oh, dear," Nancy said. "If it is William, why do you suppose he wants to see Lindsey?"

"No idea," Ms. Cole said. "He was very circumspect."

The group was silent taking this in, and Lindsey wondered if she was about to deal with an overly aggressive salesman or an aggrieved patron. Neither one of which would be good for her digestion.

"Not to make it all about me, but I have a casserole here that's getting cold," Paula said.

At the mention of food, the ladies adjusted their priorities accordingly and moved to take their seats at the table.

"Before I go out there, can I ask why the arrival of William Dorchester, if that's who this man is, is so shocking?" Lindsey asked.

Nancy looked at Ms. Cole, who nodded while spooning some of Paula's casserole onto her plate.

"Because he's the son of Marion Dorchester," Nancy said. "You know, the old lady who lives in the broken-down old mansion on the edge of town. As far as I know, he hasn't been back here since . . ."

"The runaway bride went missing," Ms. Cole said.

"I was going to say 1989," Nancy said. She looked annoyed to have her thunder stolen.

"Runaway bride?" Beth asked. She was munching on a fig in a blanket. "Tell us more."

Lindsey glanced at the clock, aware that she was keeping the man waiting. "Abridged version, please."

"William Dorchester was in love with Grace Little, but his mother, Marion, refused to let him marry Grace as she deemed her unsuitable, or more accurately too poor," Nancy said. "Grace married Timothy Hartwell instead—"

"The Little League coach?" Paula asked.

"Yes," Nancy said. "But then Grace went missing six weeks after she married Tim. He and William had a terrible fight as William accused Tim of killing Grace. Tim naturally denied it."

"How have I never heard of this?" Beth asked. "I've known Tim for years."

"There was never any proof," Ms. Cole said. "William left town, swearing to his mother that he would never marry—to spite her—and he left."

"He hasn't returned once in all these years," Nancy said. She frowned. "I wonder what brings him here now?"

Lindsey blew out a breath. "Well, I suppose I'll go find out."

Ready to find
your next great read?

Let us help.

Visit prh.com/nextread